Everyone is smitten with this series!

GIRLS ACTING
CATTY

A *Girls' Life* Must Read selection

"A humorous read of a new breed many girls will
relate to." —*Girls' Life*

"This book remind[s] me of those by Judy Blume
and Beverly Cleary." —*The Examiner*

BOYS ARE
DOGS

"Fresh, fun, and full of heart."
—Meg Cabot, bestselling author of the Princess Diaries
and Allie Finkle's Rules for Girls series

"Sweeties, you *must* read this wonderful book.
IT HAS SO MUCH GREAT ADVICE ABOUT BOYS IN IT!!!!!"
—Lauren Myracle, bestselling author of *Eleven*, *Twelve*,
and *Thirteen*

★ "[An] effervescent story. . . . Margolis gets the details
of middle-school boy behavior just right. . . . A thoughtful story
along with, just possibly, some substantive boy advice."
—*Publishers Weekly*, starred review

Books by
Leslie Margolis

The Annabelle Unleashed series

Boys Are Dogs
Girls Acting Catty
Everybody Bugs Out
One Tough Chick

❧

The Maggie Brooklyn Mysteries

Girl's Best Friend
Vanishing Acts

GIRLS ACTING CATTY

Leslie Margolis

BLOOMSBURY
NEW YORK   LONDON   NEW DELHI   SYDNEY

First published in the United States of America in November 2009
by Bloomsbury Children's Books
Paperback edition published in September 2010
www.bloomsbury.com

For information about permission to reproduce selections from this book, write to
Permissions, Bloomsbury Children's Books, 175 Fifth Avenue, New York, New York 10010

The Library of Congress has cataloged the hardcover edition as follows:
Margolis, Leslie.
Girls acting catty / Leslie Margolis.—1st U.S. ed.
p.   cm.
Summary: Sixth-grader Annabelle spends autumn coping with competing groups of friends
at school, her mother's pre-wedding stress, learning to get along with a cute stepbrother-
to-be, and such momentous events as wearing her first bra and learning to shave her legs.
ISBN-13: 978-1-59990-237-1 • ISBN-10: 1-59990-237-0 (hardcover)
[1. Interpersonal relations—Fiction. 2. Remarriage—Fiction. 3. Middle schools—Fiction.
4. Schools—Fiction. 5. Family life—California—Fiction. 6. California—Fiction.] I. Title.
PZ7.M33568Gir 2009   [Fic]—dc22   2009002144

ISBN 978-1-59990-520-4 (paperback)

Book design by Nicole Gastonguay
Typeset by Westchester Book Composition
Printed in the U.S.A. by Thomson-Shore, Dexter, Michigan
5 7 9 10 8 6

All papers used by Bloomsbury Publishing, Inc., are natural, recyclable products
made from wood grown in well-managed forests. The manufacturing processes
conform to the environmental regulations of the country of origin.

For my mom

GiRLS acTiNG
CaTTY

chapter one
time flies and so do eggs

The last half hour of daylight before Halloween night has got to be the longest stretch of time in the history of the world.

"Is it five thirty yet?" Claire asked as she paced back and forth across my living room.

Emma looked up from her map. "No, it's only forty-five seconds later than when you last asked."

"Ugh! I can't take it anymore," said Claire.

The rest of us groaned. This really was torture. The sun just wouldn't set fast enough. Getting through a full day of classes had been hard enough. Some of our teachers made the mistake of giving us actual work, but everyone was too hyped up on sugar to focus. They should've known better. Trying to teach on Halloween was like trying to teach on the last day of school: scientifically impossible.

The halls swarmed with witches and wizards, pirates and peacocks, lions and tigers and bears, oh mice, two ferrets, a bunch of hippies, and a handful of superheroes.

Not to sound braggy, but my friends and I had the coolest, most unique costumes in the entire sixth grade. We went as exotic fish—the saltwater variety. We got the idea two weeks ago when we were hanging out at Yumi's. Her parents have this huge tank in their living room, with a ton of super-rare, colorful creatures that come from all over the world.

We made everything ourselves out of silk and gauze and bendable wire. Claire showed us what to do, mostly. It was easy for her, since she makes a lot of her own clothes anyway, or at least improves them—adding beads and embroidery to her basic jeans and T-shirts. She went as a dartfish, decked out in purple and orange silk to match her red hair. She trimmed her entire costume in silver sequins so it'd shimmer as if she really were underwater.

Yumi went as a black-and-white-spotted triggerfish. Since they sometimes bite, she also wore a pair of vampire fangs.

Emma went as a yellow sea horse. And I was something called the Scott's fairy wrasse, which I chose because it's so colorful.

Rachel didn't want to be a fish, so she went as the pink castle in the tank that the rest of the fish swim through. We helped her paint a cardboard box, and cut out a drawbridge and turrets and everything.

"I can't get over how adorable you girls look," said my mom as she came into the living room.

"Mom!" I knew it was true, but it was embarrassing that she'd said so. Especially since she happened to be wearing a black pointy hat, a purple wig, and a long, warty green nose. At least she wasn't going trick-or-treating with us. As a sixth grader, I was finally allowed to go with only friends and no parents. She just had the costume on so she could answer the door for other kids. Which was nice. I guess.

I reached for a mini Snickers bar from the huge bowl in Mom's hand, but she held it over her head. "Sorry, Annabelle. You can't trick-or-treat in your own house."

"But my friends don't live here. You can't feed them and expect me to starve."

Mom sighed. "Fine, but only one piece each." As soon as she lowered the bowl we all swarmed.

Ever notice how eating candy just makes you crave more candy? It's a never-ending cycle.

Suddenly my dog, Pepper, barked and raced for the door. A second later, the doorbell rang.

"Oh no! We were supposed to be the first ones out on the street," Rachel cried.

"Hurry up," said Emma, as we scrambled for our pillowcases.

We pushed past my mom, who opened the door to a bunch of pint-size princesses. Phew! For a second I worried we'd have real competition.

"Have fun, girls," Mom called, as we raced next door. "And be careful."

After three houses, Rachel tried crossing the street but Emma stopped her. "Wait, that's the wrong way."

"But my parents got Reese's Pieces," said Rachel.

"We'll go to your house later. Otherwise, we'll have to backtrack and lose precious time. Trust me. I've figured it all out, remember?" Emma waved her map. She'd found the route that would best "maximize our candy acquisition potential." At least I think that's how she put it.

Emma is a brainiac—one of those straight-A students who reads the dictionary for fun and always does extra credit, even though she's the last person ever to need it. Sometimes she's hard to follow. But we all knew it was best to let her lead.

We raced from door to door to door on my side of the street, and then the next. Six blocks later, when we were at the corner across from the local elementary school, Emma said it was time to turn around.

"But I heard they're giving away king-size chocolate bars in Canyon Ranch," said Rachel.

Canyon Ranch was the rich side of town, just past the school. All the houses there had four- or five-car garages and big iron gates. Some were even three stories high.

"People say that every year but it's not true," said Emma. "Anyway, we'll get more candy by hitting a lot of houses faster, and there are four more houses per square block on this side of town. Plus, they're closer to the sidewalk, which means less walking."

"Wait, you actually counted?" asked Yumi.

"And measured?" Claire added.

"I didn't have to." Emma shrugged. "All the information was available online, so it was just a matter of plugging numbers into a mathematical equation."

I was impressed. Sure we made fun of Emma for plotting everything out so carefully, but an hour later, we were back where we started with full pillowcases.

"Let's dump out the candy at Annabelle's and start over," said Emma. "People will be more sympathetic if we show up with empty bags."

"Good thinking," said Claire.

We headed for my house but didn't make it very far, because a group of kids blocked our path. The closest streetlight was out, so I couldn't really see them clearly. And it didn't help that they were dressed in all black, with dark scarves covering the bottom half of their faces.

"Where do you think you're going?" asked a menacing and all-too-familiar-sounding voice.

Uh-oh.

I clutched my pillowcase tightly and took a step back. The group moved in closer. Once my eyes adjusted to the dark, I recognized them. They were eighth-grade boys dressed as ninjas. And they carried dangerous weapons: eggs.

Yes. An egg is a dangerous weapon. If you've ever faced a breakfast-themed firing squad, you know exactly what I'm talking about.

But there's something even worse than being

outnumbered by a bunch of eighth-grade ninjas carrying eggs—being outnumbered by a bunch of eighth-grade ninjas carrying eggs, when one of those ninjas happens to be Jackson.

Tall, with spiky blond hair and a mischievous grin, he stood in the center of the group. Like he called all the shots, which was so typical.

I had only moved here two months ago, but that was more than enough time to figure out that Jackson was the human equivalent of a major tornado—shaking things up and doing tons of damage wherever he went. And it's not like I could avoid him, either. Jackson lives across the street from me, but even worse—he's Rachel's older brother.

There was only one thing to do in this situation. "Run!" I yelled, and bolted. Luckily my friends took my advice. We scattered in five different directions.

Sure, we were outnumbered. But we were fast.

Well, most of us were fast.

I managed to duck behind a tree, while Yumi and Claire hid behind a parked car. Poor Emma lagged and got hit in the shoulder.

Then someone whacked Rachel in the back. "Jackson! I'm telling," she screamed, which just attracted more ninjas.

Rachel headed my way with four boys trailing close behind, so I ran across the street and ducked behind my neighbor's hedges. The boys' sneaker soles pounded against the pavement, their thumps matching my racing heart.

A few seconds later, I noticed a pink cardboard blur—Rachel running into my backyard. Emma and Yumi made it there too. I was about to join them when I spotted Claire in Rachel's driveway, backed up against the garage door and surrounded by three boys, all of them armed and dangerous.

I couldn't leave her stranded so I ran over, yelling, "No, don't!"

They turned around and stared at me like I was nuts. But I wasn't. I had a plan. Okay, not quite a plan. But I did have an idea.

Let me explain. Like I mentioned before, I had just moved to town. I used to go to an all-girls school. And going to school with boys? It's a lot different.

At first, the boys at Birchwood Middle School seemed like an alien species. They didn't have glow-in-the-dark skin, enormous foreheads, or those gigantic black holes for eyes or anything. It was more about how they acted—yelling out random stuff in class, kicking my chair, eating really disgusting food and then having burping contests. It was totally shocking, and not in a good way.

To make matters worse, my new dog, Pepper, was wild and out of control too.

But then I started reading up on dog training, and teaching Pepper how to behave, and that's when I figured something out.

Boys and dogs have a lot in common. They don't always know how to act, instinctually. Sometimes they need to be told what to do. Except you can't just tell them straight out. You have to talk to them in a certain way. So when I approached the guys in Rachel's driveway, I stood tall, looked each of them in the eye, and spoke firmly.

"Leave her alone," I said. And they listened.

Claire was now safe. There was just one small problem. Now they aimed their eggs at me.

Jackson laughed meanly.

Luckily, I remembered something else that dogs and boys share: short-term memories. "Um, you know they have king-size chocolate bars at the Wiggenses' house," I tried.

"Really?" asked one of the ninjas.

"Dude, don't let her distract you," Jackson said as he swung his arm like a baseball pitcher warming up, but in slow motion.

Claire looked at me with wide blue eyes. Her braid was half undone, and loose strands of red hair floated around her flushed cheeks. "You know their eggs are rotten, right?" she whispered.

I gulped and repeated one of the dog-training lessons in my head. *Never show fear. A dog that thinks you're afraid of him is never going to respect you.*

I hid my shaking hands behind my back and shrugged, copping my best "relaxed and casual" pose. "Maybe I'm lying and maybe I'm not. You really want to take that risk?"

"Which house is the Wiggenses'?" one of the ninjas asked.

"Second in from the corner across the street. The one with the lawn gnome."

Two ninjas gazed at the house hungrily.

"Don't listen to her," said Jackson, but it was too late. They were already gone—moving as fast as Pepper had the other day when I dropped some goldfish on the kitchen floor. (The crackers, not the fish.)

Now it was me and Claire against Jackson. He was outnumbered, but still armed.

"Sneaky," said Jackson.

I shrugged and tried not to smile. "I call it self-defense."

"Everyone knows they'd only give out king-size chocolate in Canyon Ranch, and even that's probably not true."

Yes, the guy was annoying, but he wasn't completely clueless.

"Okay, fine," I admitted. "The Wiggenses aren't even home. But who knows? Maybe they do have giant chocolate bars at their house. I never said they were passing them out. I just said they *had* them, which is entirely possible."

He smirked and wound up again. "Oh, Spaz, you are gonna be sorry."

I grabbed Claire's arm. "We're going to back away slowly," I said, as if we were in the middle of a hostage situation. "And you're going to let us leave."

Jackson paused. "You think I'd waste this perfectly good egg?"

I narrowed my eyes at him. "If you ruin our costumes, if you get even one trace of rotten egg on us, I'll get you back, twice as bad."

"And how would you manage that?" he scoffed, disbelieving.

I tried to look intimidating. Unfortunately, I'm kind of shrimpy—short and blond and skinny too. Not exactly built to intimidate an eighth grader or even a sixth-grade boy. Maybe I could intimidate a small third grader, but why would I want to? That would be cruel. "I'm not telling, but trust me, you'll be sorry."

"Real sorry," Claire added.

"Yeah, right," Jackson said, all sarcastic.

Claire and I had to escape. Pretty soon those two ninja dudes would figure out I was lying about the Wiggenses' place, and then we'd be toast. Eggy toast. And I don't mean the French variety.

Suddenly Claire pointed over Jackson's shoulder and yelled, "Oh my gosh—it's a vampire bat!"

When he turned around to look, Claire sprang forward, grabbed the egg right out of his hand, and smashed it over his head.

"What the—"

Before Jackson could finish his sentence, we were gone, sprinting across the street to safety.

Yumi, Rachel, and Emma were waiting for us in the backyard—so giddy and excited they were jumping up and down.

"I can't believe you egged my brother. That's too excellent!" said Rachel.

"What did you say to him, anyway?" asked Emma.

"Yeah, tell us everything," said Yumi.

After Claire finished the story, we peeked out front. As far as we could tell, the ninjas had moved on.

"Do you guys want to change before we head back out?" I asked, since the egg attack had left Emma and Rachel slightly stinky.

"There's no time," said Emma. "Plus, we don't have new costumes to change into. Can you guys stand the smell for another half hour?"

"Sure. It's no biggie," I said. "What are friends for?"

We continued trick-or-treating, and even got sympathy points (meaning extra candy) when we told this old man we'd been attacked by rotten-egg-wielding ninjas. So it was totally worth it. We were just debating whether or not we could hit our favorite spots a second time, when Rachel stopped in her tracks and whispered, "Yikes."

I looked around, but didn't see Jackson or his friends anywhere. "Where are they?" I asked.

Rachel pointed to Taylor and Hannah, two sixth graders from school. They were with two other girls I didn't know. But I could tell they were all good friends, since they had on matching costumes. Each wore a shiny purple top and tight black pants. They were covered in body glitter, and had on makeup too: purple eye shadow, dark eyeliner, and red lipstick. If

I didn't know any better, I'd have thought they were in high school. I knew it was Halloween and all, and dressing up like someone else is the point, but their costumes seemed different. Even without the body glitter, there was something sparkly about them.

"Hi!" I tried moving closer, but Rachel pulled me back.

Taylor held up her hands and scrunched up her nose. "Ew, what's that smell?" she asked.

"Um, we got egged," I said. "Some of us did, anyway, but just a little."

"And you're still, like, out here? Disgusting," said one of the girls I didn't know. She had long, dark curly hair and braces with purple rubber bands. I wondered if her bands were always purple, or if she got special ones to match her costume. I didn't ask her, though. Something about the way she glared at us—like we'd just crawled out from under a sewer grate—made me not want to speak to her.

Taylor surveyed our whole group, asking, "What are you supposed to be, anyway?"

"Exotic fish," I replied. "Except for Rachel. She's the castle in the tank."

"A castle?" Taylor asked and then smirked. "Seriously. You're a castle?"

Rachel elbowed me. Everyone else got quiet so I did too.

Taylor stared pointedly at Rachel and said, "I'm surprised you didn't find a costume that would hide your face."

Rachel's cheeks burned red. "What are you talking about?" she asked.

"If I had pimples like yours, I'd have worn a paper bag over my head," said the girl with braces. "Except not just on Halloween. I'm talking about every day."

Her friends giggled behind their hands.

"Well, at least I'm wearing a real costume," said Rachel. She tried crossing her arms over her chest but the box got in the way, which made Taylor and her friends laugh harder.

"What are you guys supposed to be, anyway?" Yumi asked.

"Rock stars, obviously. I'm so over this." Taylor rolled her eyes, turned around, and headed off, teetering slightly on her spiky heels. Her three friends trailed close behind.

Meanwhile, Rachel fumed. "Rock stars?" she yelled. "You don't even have any instruments!"

Rather than answer her, Taylor and her friends laughed. Meanly.

"Just forget about it," said Emma once they were out of earshot. "Come on, let's go."

We finally got back to trick-or-treating, and ended up with an insane amount of candy. But after the run-in with Taylor's crowd, somehow all the fun had drained out of the night.

It was weird. Facing the ninjas had been hard, and they'd posed a real threat: rotten eggs, ruined costumes, and humiliation in front of Jackson—my least favorite boy, ever.

13

All Taylor and her friends did was talk to us and look at us in a mean way. It shouldn't have mattered, but it did.

Pepper's dog-training lessons usually worked on the Birchwood boys. Yet I had this eerie feeling that, somehow, the same tricks were never going to work on a bunch of girls.

chapter two
tulips and pepper don't mix

My mom raced into the kitchen bright and early the next morning, hair unbrushed and only half dressed in jeans, a nightshirt, and fuzzy pink bunny slippers.

"Annabelle, guess what? I'm going to be a bride!" she practically yelled.

I looked up from the pile of candy I was sorting through, totally confused. For one thing, I wasn't deaf. But more importantly, Halloween was over. "Um, isn't it a little early to start planning for next year?"

My mom laughed, and I didn't even know what was so funny, or why she was in such a great mood before she'd had her morning coffee.

"Are you okay?" I asked.

"I'm better than okay. What I meant was, I'm going to be a bride in real life, because Ted and I just got engaged."

I stared at her, not really comprehending.

"To be married," she added.

"Oh." I sat back and crossed my arms over my

chest, which felt strangely tight. "Yeah, I know what engaged means."

"Well, good." She held out her hand and showed me her new ring—a thin gold band with a small diamond in the center. The stone sparkled, but not nearly as brightly as her green eyes. I hadn't seen her this excited since, well, I can't remember since when. "He surprised me with it last night."

"Wow." I tried to muster up some enthusiasm but my voice sounded flat, like a can of soda that'd been left out in the sun. I knew I should've been happy for her. So why did I feel a monster-size lump forming in my throat? And how come, when I glanced down at my candy, all the bright and shiny wrappers looked blurry?

"Oh, you're upset!" my mom cried.

"No, I'm not," I said, but she could probably tell I was bluffing, since I had to blink to keep from crying.

"I'm sorry, Annabelle. I didn't mean to spring this on you. I'm just so excited. I couldn't help myself."

She tried to put her hand over mine but I pulled it away.

"It's fine," I said. "I mean it's great. I'm, um, really happy for you." And I wanted to be, I really did. But my mom has never been married before. It's always been just the two of us. At least it was until last summer, when we moved in with her boyfriend, Ted Weeble. That's how we ended up in this big house in Westlake. Before that, Mom and I had lived in a cozy apartment in North Hollywood, thirty miles away. When Mom told me about the big move last summer, she said we'd all live together for a while to make sure we got along before she and Ted made a bigger commitment.

I'd thought that would take years, not months. "Isn't this kind of soon?" I asked.

"We *had* planned on waiting a little longer," Mom said, pulling out a chair and sitting down next to me. "But it feels right. And I know it's big news, and you've already been so wonderful about the move and—" Just then she noticed my candy. "You're not eating that for breakfast, are you?"

"I'm just sorting it. Want a piece?" I offered her a cherry Jolly Rancher—her favorite.

"No thanks." She shook her head. "Please don't worry, honey. Marriage isn't going to change anything, really, since we already all live together."

"So I noticed."

She sighed in sympathy, and tugged on her blond curls with one hand. "My point is, we've gotten through the hardest part. I know the move was a big adjustment, but you're doing so well here. And you certainly had a fun Halloween."

I shrugged, thinking again about how un-fun the night turned out to be after we ran into Taylor and her friends. Not that I was going to tell my mom about that.

"Nothing is going to change except that Ted will

be my husband, and not my boyfriend. And he'll be your stepdad too. But those are just labels, words."

Sure, my mom was trying to make me feel better, but I hadn't even thought about the whole stepdad factor. I'd never had a real dad. Not one I've ever met, anyway. And now I'd have a stepdad? I didn't know what to make of it, so I went back to counting my candy: three Gobstoppers, six packets of SweeTarts, and four ropes of licorice. No, make that five. Three were red and two were black. I can't stand licorice.

"We'll have a small ceremony in the backyard, probably. I'm thinking very low-key, but Ted wants something traditional. We're still working that out. Oh, and I need to ask you something. Will you be my maid of honor?"

She'd made me lose count. Now I couldn't remember if I had six boxes of Junior Mints or seven.

"Annabelle?"

"Hold on a sec." It was eight boxes, actually.

"Did you hear me?" she asked.

"Yup."

She placed her palms on the table and leaned in closer. "Yes, you heard me? Or yes, you'll be my maid of honor?"

"Yes to both," I said, and finally looked up at her. "But does that mean I have to get all dressed up?"

I felt bad as soon as the words left my mouth. Especially when I noticed Mom's smile fade. "Just kidding," I said, even though I wasn't, completely.

My uncle, Jake, and his boyfriend, Shane, had a

commitment ceremony two years ago. Mom made me wear a yellow dress *and* itchy tights *and* patent leather shoes that pinched my toes and left me with three blisters. It was ridiculously annoying—the outfit, that is. The ceremony was fine, a little boring, but worth it in the end because they served pigs in a blanket afterward, with three different kinds of mustard.

"I'll take you shopping for a dress, but we can talk about that later," my mom said. "I won't force you into doing anything you don't want to do."

"Like how you didn't force me into moving here," I mumbled.

She ignored that last comment. "Ted is out running, but I was thinking, when he gets back, maybe we can all do something fun."

It seemed like Ted was always out for a run. He's in training for the LA Marathon, which means he'll have to run 26.2 miles, all at once, this spring. I'm still not sure why.

"But I'm sleeping over at Yumi's tonight. I can still go, right?"

"Of course you can, but we have all day."

I put away my candy. Most went into the pantry, but I kept some in the pillowcase, so I could take it to Yumi's later. Rachel, Claire, and Emma were sleeping over there too, and we planned to trade whatever we didn't want.

"Today's not so great, actually. I have a lot to do. Homework and stuff." I hurried out of the kitchen.

My mom called for me, but I was already halfway

up the stairs and pretended like I didn't hear her. She knocked on my door a few minutes later to see if I wanted to talk, but I was afraid that if I tried, I'd start crying, so I said no and hid in my room all day.

I didn't go downstairs until four o'clock, when Rachel came over. Mom drove us both to Yumi's, and luckily she didn't bring up the wedding again.

By the time we arrived, Claire and Emma were already there so we got down to candy-swapping right away.

I'd brought all my chewy stuff, which I don't like because it sticks to my molars, and leaves a bad aftertaste. Luckily, SweeTarts are too sour for Claire, so she took all my licorice instead. And Rachel is allergic to coconut so we traded my caramels for her Almond Joys.

By the time we finished, our pizza had arrived. After dinner, we played Monopoly but as usual, the game got boring after about an hour (that's why they're called *board* games, I think) so we switched to Dance Dance Revolution.

When that got old, Yumi said, "Can you believe how awful Terrible T looked last night?"

"Terrible T?" I asked.

"That's what we call Taylor Stansfield," Rachel told me. "She's Terrible T and her friends are the Three Terrors."

"We used to call them Triplicate Terrors," Emma explained. "But it's too much of a tongue twister."

"They were like zombie clones, but with too much makeup," said Rachel. "Which makes sense, since they act like clones."

"Or sheep," said Emma. "They should've dressed up as Dolly. It would've been more accurate."

"Huh?" I asked.

"Dolly, the sheep. She was the first animal ever to be cloned. It happened in Scotland in 1996," Emma explained. "She only lived for six years, though."

"Our costumes were way better," said Yumi. "No question."

"They weren't even dressed up, really," said Claire. "I mean other than the body glitter, they'd all wear those outfits to school."

"Yeah, I'm sure Taylor thinks she's too cool to wear a real costume," said Rachel. She flopped back into the couch like she was so annoyed she couldn't even sit up straight. "She and her friends all think they're so fabulous, but I don't know why they're so popular. She's not even that pretty, you know?"

Rachel looked at me but I had nothing to add. I'd spent so much time this fall dealing with all the troublesome boys, I'd never even given much thought to the other girls at Birchwood. I hadn't needed to, since I was lucky enough to move into the house across the street from Rachel. We met before school started, and she introduced me to Claire, Emma, and Yumi, and we've all been hanging out ever since. It's like I just fit in perfectly from day one.

"Wait, you don't actually *like* Taylor and her friends, do you?" Rachel asked me.

"I don't know them," I said, not quite answering her question, and hoping she wouldn't press the issue. Because the truth was, until I saw how mean Taylor was to Rachel last night, I'd thought she was cool. And not just her—I had a couple of classes with Hannah too. The three of us sat together in chorus. Sometimes we talked before and after class, and we always smiled when we passed one another in the halls. We weren't friends, exactly, but we weren't not friends, either. And we definitely weren't enemies.

"Trust me. If you did know them, you wouldn't like them," said Rachel. She had this funny expression on her face, like she'd eaten too many Sour Patch Kids. Which was entirely possible, but I don't think that was it. I hadn't seen Rachel so angry before—not even at Jackson.

"Hey, let's watch the movie now," I said, anxious to change the subject.

Yumi had rented *High School Musical III*. Since it was pretty late, we set up our sleeping bags in front of the TV before we watched. Apparently, only Yumi and Claire made it through to the end of the movie. Or so they said. When we woke up the next morning, the TV was still on, so I had my doubts.

Back home, I found my mom and Dweeble planting tulips in the yard.

Dweeble is what I sometimes call Ted, my mom's

boyfriend—I mean, fiancé. I know I shouldn't, but sometimes he makes it hard not to, like this morning. He had on a gigantic floppy sun hat. Okay yes, Dweeble is over six feet tall and bald, so he probably has to be extra-careful about sunburn, since his bare head is closer to the sun than most people's. But still . . . Hasn't he ever heard of a baseball cap?

As much as I wanted to sneak upstairs, I knew I couldn't hide out forever. My mom would wonder where I was, and when she found out I was alone in my room, again, she'd probably want to talk about my feelings, and I wasn't in the mood. So I walked outside.

Pepper bounded toward me, planting his dirty paws on my legs. "Hey, guy." I scratched him behind his ears. His black-and-white shaggy fur was caked in dirt, but I didn't care. "Miss me?" I bent down so he could lick my face.

Not even his bad breath bothered me. That's how much I loved my dog.

Mom stood up, shaded her eyes from the sun, and squinted. "Hi, Annabelle. How was Yumi's?"

"It was fun."

"Do you like the new flowers?" She gestured toward two rows of red and yellow tulips.

"Um, sure." I shrugged.

"We're putting these in now so we can see how they'll look for the wedding. We're not sure if we should go with tulips or roses or African violets. Oh, and we finally picked a date." Mom wiped some sweat off her brow, leaving behind a muddy streak. "December fifteenth."

I slapped my forehead with the palm of my hand. "But that's when I plan on rearranging my sock drawer!"

"Cute," Mom replied, although she didn't seem to think it was.

"I wanted to wait until June so we'd have more time to plan," Dweeble said. "But your mother insisted, and she's the boss."

"So that's how it's going to be?" My mom giggled and swatted Dweeble's knee with one of her gardening gloves.

Ugh. There's nothing worse than witnessing my mom flirt with Dweeble. Luckily, she snapped out of it pretty quickly and turned to me. "My thinking is, why wait? There's not much to plan. The point is to be married, not to have a wedding, which is why we're going to have a low-key ceremony in the backyard."

"Also your mom's idea. And guess what?" Dweeble asked, and then answered before I even had a chance to guess. "You'll finally get to meet Jason. He has a long winter break, so he'll be here for Thanksgiving and the whole month of December, practically."

"And he's staying here?" I asked.

"Of course."

Jason is Dweeble's son from his first marriage. He's really old—twenty, I think—and he's going to college in Switzerland this year. I wondered if he was dweeby too. Probably, since he had the same last name, and half the same genes. I decided to call him mini-Dweeb, but not out loud, of course.

"Oh, and you can invite one friend to the wedding," said my mom.

"Just one?" I asked.

"Yes, because we're trying to keep it small."

"Okay, cool," I said. And then, since I didn't want them to try and rope me into helping out with the planting, I headed inside and up to my room.

Dweeble grilled steaks for dinner that night to celebrate the engagement. I thought that's what the wedding was for, but whatever. I wasn't going to complain because they were really good. He also made his famous mashed potatoes. His words—I still don't know why they're famous, but they're so tasty, I'm not going to ask.

They asked me more about Halloween and school and the sleepover, but mostly they talked about the wedding. Boring stuff, like how they had to choose a caterer, and figure out what kind of music they wanted, and then there was the guest list.

Yawn! It was hard to stay awake—and not just because I'd gotten less than four hours of sleep at Yumi's last night. In fact, I must've drifted off at the table, because suddenly I heard my mom yelling, "Pepper, what did you do?"

My eyes snapped open just in time to see my dog

dragging a huge clump of yellow tulips into the dining room, and trailing lots of mud in the process. He looked so proud of himself that I had to smile.

No one else thought he was so cute, though. My mom jumped up from the table and headed outside while Dweeble and I followed.

Yellow and red petals littered the lawn. Pepper had torn out half the new flowers.

"All that hard work!" said my mom. "What a waste!"

"I guess we'll have to put up fencing next time," said Dweeble.

"But that won't look nice. Someone needs to train him not to dig." My mom looked at me, which *so* wasn't fair.

Sure, technically Pepper's my dog. But I'm not the one who needed a fancy backyard for a wedding.

Maybe Pepper wasn't so psyched about the marriage, either, and this was his way of protesting. If so, I had to give him credit for taking action.

All I'd done was sulk about it.

chapter three
terrible t

When I got to PE on Monday, I sat down on the blacktop for roll call, as usual. We always line up in alphabetical order, which means that I sit right behind Taylor, because my last name is Stevens and hers is Stansfield. Usually I smile at her and she smiles back.

But ever since Halloween, I didn't know how to act. I wasn't going to *not* be nice to Taylor, just because Rachel and my other friends didn't like her. That wouldn't be fair. Sure, Taylor had been pretty mean to Rachel, but Rachel had been mean right back. I didn't know who started the whole thing, and I didn't want to get stuck in the middle or take sides.

Plus, Rachel was wrong. Taylor isn't ugly. She's actually really pretty, with shiny dark hair and wide-set green eyes. Also, she's super outgoing. In chorus, she's always the first one to volunteer to do solos. She wants to be a pop star when she grows up, and she talks about it all the time. Rachel thinks this makes her obnoxious and snobby, but I think it's okay to have something you really, really want to do.

Rachel should agree. She's the one who wants to be a drummer in a rock band. So how is that any different? I'd asked her about it on Saturday night, but she didn't explain and I didn't push it.

To smile or not to smile—that was the question. Before I could decide, Taylor turned around and looked at me with a blank expression on her face, like she was just noticing I existed for the first time. That seemed a little weird, but then she did something really crazy. She panned my whole body, looking me up and down like I was a secondhand bike she was thinking about buying. When she finally finished she looked disappointed, and frowned like she thought I was used and damaged goods.

"What?" I shouldn't have asked, but the question came out before I could stop myself.

She scrunched her eyebrows together, as if she were thinking pretty hard, which got me all panicky. Like, maybe she found so many things wrong, she didn't even know where to begin.

When her gaze finally met mine she asked, "Your mom won't let you shave your legs yet, huh?"

I looked down at my legs, and she did too. I didn't know what to tell her, or even if I was supposed to give her an answer.

True, my legs are a little furry, but my hair is so pale you can hardly see it. There's no point in shaving. But what if every other sixth-grade girl at Birchwood already does? Maybe I'm the only hold-out.

I'm not sure if Rachel or my other new friends shaved. We'd never talked about it before. Maybe they all did and thought I was weird and babyish for not doing it. Although they were my friends, and too nice to think of me that way. So maybe they didn't bring up shaving on purpose because they didn't want me to feel bad, which was worse.

I sat there dumbly, looking at my legs. Time seemed to slow to a crawl. Each agonizing second felt more like an hour.

Taylor stared at me, waiting for an answer. She didn't even blink.

Finally I said, "No." But even as the word came out of my mouth, I wished I'd had a better response.

Like, "I'm not sure, because I don't want to shave my legs yet, so I never bothered asking. But if I did, my mom would probably say go ahead, because she's cool about stuff like that."

That was the truth. But the truth didn't seem good enough. Of course, neither did the lie. Taylor turned back around and didn't say anything else to me for the rest of class.

Probably, she'd never speak to me again.

At this point, I kind of hoped not.

PE is my last class of the day, but I couldn't go right home when it ended because I had to meet

Tobias and Oliver in the library after school. We're in the same lab group in science, and we'd spent the last two weeks growing mold spores on bread. Now we had to write up a lab report about the experiment. It was due on Wednesday, and these reports counted for a big part of our grade, so we really had to get it right.

I just wished I had long pants to change into. I'd worn shorts to school and tennis shoes with no socks. Now I worried that everyone would notice my hairy calves and think I was a freak. It was entirely possible that I was the only girl at Birchwood Middle School who didn't shave. And until I knew for sure, I'd just have to be careful to keep my legs hidden.

When I got to the library, the boys were already there. Oliver is cute, with dirty blond hair shaved into a buzz cut, green eyes, and skin that's kind of dark because he's half black. He has a nice accent, which I never noticed before, because he hardly talks. But ever since he told me he was born in Jamaica and only moved to California four years ago, I always hear it. Tobias is pale, with shaggy dark hair and glasses and a big nose and pimples that creep from his cheeks down to his neck, and disappear into his shirt collar. Basically, he's not so cute, but he seems to think he is.

Even though I was feeling lousy after the whole Taylor/leg-shaving thing, I stood up tall and swaggered over to them, throwing my backpack on the table and saying, "Hey, what's up?"

Then I pulled out my notebook and doled out the work before they had a chance to argue with me. "There are six sections in a lab, so let's split them up and each do two. Tobias, you can write the introduction and hypothesis. Oliver, you list the materials and supplies and then explain the procedure. And I'll write up our observations and the conclusion."

"How come you get to do the conclusion?" asked Tobias.

I crossed my arms over my chest and glared. "Do you want to do it? Because I don't really care."

"No, whatever. It's fine." Tobias pushed up his glasses, bent over his notebook, and started writing.

I had to smile. If someone didn't know better, they'd think I was pretty bossy, but I'm not. Really. It's all an act.

At the beginning of the school year, Oliver and Tobias hogged all the lab equipment and they never let me do anything, but then I used some of Pepper's dog-training lessons on them and things have been okay ever since. For everyone, I think. We finished writing up our lab in less than two hours. Then Oliver's mom drove us all home.

I was so glad to be back. At least until I walked through the front door and heard loud voices coming from the kitchen.

"This isn't a big deal," Dweeble said. "I'm sorry,

but I just assumed that you'd want to change your name when we got married. Traditionally—"

"When have I ever been traditional?" Mom asked. "And what about Annabelle? I can't have a different last name than my own daughter."

"You didn't let me finish. I was about to say that I never thought about that, but—"

"Well, you should have."

"There you go, interrupting me again."

Yikes. I froze, just inside the front door, not wanting to eavesdrop but too curious to move. I'd never heard Mom and Dweeble fight before, and wondered if they were breaking up. They'd have to call off the wedding. Then Mom and I might have to move back to North Hollywood. I'd just gotten used to things here, and I didn't want to move. Not even after the humiliation in gym class.

I opened the door again, and slammed it shut as hard as I could, yelling, "Hi, I'm home!"

They stopped talking immediately, and then a few seconds later my mom came into the entryway with a tight, forced-looking smile on her face. "Hi, Annabelle. Did you finish your book report?"

"It's a lab report," I replied. "Um, can I ask you something?" I needed to talk to her about shaving. Not only because of what happened in PE today, but also because I was curious. I wasn't *only* asking because of Taylor. "It's important," I said, making my way upstairs and hoping she'd come too.

"What is it?" She glanced toward the kitchen, distracted. I wasn't going to ask her out in the open, when Dweeble could walk in at any second. But she wasn't following me to my room. So instead, I asked her if I could go over to Rachel's.

Mom glanced at her watch. "That's fine, but don't stay for too long. Ted and I are making lasagna and it should be ready in about an hour."

I felt like asking her if "making lasagna" was some new term for "yelling at each other," but I didn't want her to know I'd heard anything. So instead I said, "Okay." Then I dropped my backpack off in my room, changed into jeans, and headed across the street.

Jackson answered the door a minute after I knocked, asking, "What do you want?"

For once, I didn't blame him for being rude. He was probably still mad about Halloween. "Hey, Jackson. I just wanted to see if you needed to borrow my shampoo."

"Huh?" he asked.

"So you can wash all that rotten egg out of your hair. Remember? Or did Claire hit you too hard and give you amnesia?"

"Very funny," Jackson grumbled, and tried closing the door in my face.

I held it open. "No, wait. Sorry. I'm just kidding. Is Rachel home?"

Jackson rolled his eyes, but still turned around and yelled for her. "Hey, pizza face!"

I cringed. Poor Rachel. It was bad enough having bad acne, probably, without having some mean older brother making fun of her all the time.

Not that Rachel was going to sit there quietly and take it. "Shut up, egghead," she said, running downstairs. "Don't call me that."

"Why, are you going to tell on me?" Jackson asked, in a fake-whiny voice.

Rachel pushed past him. "Hey, Annabelle. Come on in."

She grabbed my arm and led me upstairs to her room.

"You are so lucky you're an only child," she said, slamming the door so we could have some privacy.

"Except I won't be for long. Pretty soon I'll have a stepbrother."

"But he's not going to live with you," said Rachel.

"He is for six weeks," I said. "Dweeble bought new sheets for the bed in the extra bedroom. In fact, he doesn't even call it the extra bedroom, anymore. Suddenly it's Jason's room. And guess what else? When mini-Dweeb stays with us, I'm going to have to share a bathroom with him."

"Mini-Dweeb?" she asked.

"That's his new nickname. It's easier to say than 'son of the Dweeb.'"

"Good point." Rachel nodded. "But I really don't think you have to worry. Mini-Dweeb is in college, which means he's too grown up to make fun of you."

This made sense, but I hadn't come over to Rachel's house to talk about brothers—real or step. "Hey, do you shave your legs?" I asked.

"Yeah," said Rachel. "I started to this summer. How come?"

She sounded so casual about it, I almost regretted bringing it up. But it was too late. I had to know. I took a deep breath and asked, "Does everyone shave their legs? All our friends, I mean."

"Um, I know Emma does, but I don't think Claire and Yumi do. How come?"

"No reason," I said. "I was just wondering." And since she was looking at me kind of funny, I told her about what happened in PE.

Rachel freaked. "I can't believe Taylor said that to you! She's so horrible!"

I nodded. It felt good, having Rachel leap to my defense so quickly. But at the same time, I didn't want to make *too* big a deal out of it.

"The thing is—I'm not positive she said it to be mean. She just sort of asked me, like she was wondering, but I don't know. It was weird . . ."

"Of course she said it to be mean," said Rachel. "That's what she's all about. Other people play instruments, or collect puffy stickers. Taylor's favorite pastime is making people feel bad about themselves. It's, like, a hobby for her. As if she's so perfect. Did you see her jeans today? They probably cost two hundred dollars, because she only wears designer clothes. But they look terrible. She should not be wearing low riders with her body because when she sat down, her shirt rode up and she had a total muffin top."

"Muffin top?" I asked.

"It's when your hips sort of swell and hang out of your jeans, like the top of a muffin."

I laughed. Sure it was mean, but it was still funny. And anyway, why should I feel bad when Taylor made me feel lousy on purpose?

"Her muffin top shows in her PE clothes too," I said. "And the other day, her underwear was sticking out of her shorts."

"No!" yelled Rachel.

"Seriously. They were pink with white stars."

"Stars?" asked Rachel. "Think she wore them because she's so convinced she's gonna be this huge star?"

We both giggled.

"She probably had them showing on purpose," Rachel said. "You know, to get attention. All her friends are like that. Don't you hate how they walk around school like they own it? They're the biggest snobs in the entire sixth grade and, like, proud of it."

I didn't know any of Taylor's friends except for Hannah, who I'd always liked. She and I sat next to each other in French. She's tall, with big brown eyes and straight, shoulder-length dirty-blond hair that she constantly tucks and re-tucks behind her ears. Whenever we have to switch papers for grading in French, we choose each other. Last Tuesday, I got a hundred percent and she put a happy face by my score.

Snobby girls do not draw happy faces. It's a fact.

"Hannah seems okay," I said.

Rachel groaned. "Hannah is the worst! She pretends like she's all sweet and quiet, but it's just an act. Trust me. If she were nice, she wouldn't be friends with Taylor. Haven't you noticed how she follows her around and does whatever she wants like some clueless, pathetic little puppet?"

I shrugged. "I guess I never really paid attention."

"Well, now that I pointed it out I know you'll notice. And you cannot start shaving now, just because of what Taylor said."

I didn't know when I'd start shaving, but it didn't seem like the kind of thing Rachel should be able to decide for me. I mean, I'm glad she was on my side and everything, but she was acting weird—too angry for something that didn't even happen to her.

"But what if my legs are too hairy? People are noticing, obviously."

"Let's see."

I rolled up my jeans and Rachel leaned closer to inspect my calves. "Your hair is so pale, you can hardly see it."

"That's what I used to think."

"You know, once you start shaving you can never stop. Your hair won't be all soft and smooth like it is now."

"It won't?" I rolled my jeans back down and crossed my legs.

Rachel shook her head. "Nope. The razor cuts it at a different angle, so it'll feel all stubbly. My mom waxes, but waxing looks like torture."

My only experience with wax involved wax lips, but somehow I doubted that's what Rachel was talking about. "What's waxing?" I asked.

"It's when they brush hot wax on your legs and then cover it with cloth. When the wax cools down it sticks to your hair and then they rip the cloth off really fast and it takes the wax and all your hair with it."

I gasped. "No!"

"Seriously. It's totally painful, because it rips the hair out from the follicles," Rachel explained. "But it lasts longer, for the same reason."

"It doesn't take your skin off with it?" I asked.

Rachel shook her head. "Nope. But I'd still never do it. Shaving is much better."

I didn't want to admit it out loud, but shaving didn't seem so much better to me. I know it's not supposed to hurt, but it still involves running a razor blade up your leg, and I just don't get how that can't be painful.

Ever notice how commercials for razor blades always feature some woman shaving in a gigantic tub filled with bubble bath? Well, bubble bath makes me sneeze. So what happens if I sneeze and slip and cut myself with the razor? I'd start to bleed, probably, and blood makes me squeamish. What if I'm bleeding and the sight of it makes me pass out? I could drown in my very own bathtub. That is not a good way to go. Not that there's any good way to go, but drowning in your own bathwater has got to be one of the worst.

I guess Rachel could tell I was stressing, because she said, "You don't need to shave. Just forget about Taylor. I wish we didn't have PE with her. I wish she didn't even go to our school."

"Yeah." I agreed because it was easier, but to be honest, Taylor hadn't ever really bugged me much before. Well, except for today. And on Halloween, I guess.

I wondered why Rachel hated Taylor so much, but that wasn't something I could just ask her straight out.

On my way home, I had this weird thought. Maybe Taylor made me feel bad on purpose just because I was a part of Rachel's crowd. And as for all those times she'd been nice in the past? Maybe she hadn't noticed who my friends were.

Dweeble was just taking the lasagna out of the oven when I walked inside. He and my mom acted normal for the rest of the night, so either they'd made up or they were really good at faking getting along.

As I got ready for bed, I realized I'd forgotten to ask Rachel not to say anything to our other friends. About the whole Taylor/shaving thing, I mean. I didn't want it to turn into a big deal, nor did I want to advertise that I hadn't started shaving, but it was too late to call her. And by the time I saw her again, she'd already spilled the beans.

At school the next morning I found all my friends huddled around my locker. As soon as I was close enough, Emma said, "I can't believe Taylor said that to you."

I looked from her to Rachel to Claire to Yumi. "What's going on?" I asked, although I already had a pretty good idea.

"I told them how Terrible T made fun of you for not shaving," said Rachel.

"She didn't make fun of me exactly," I said as I worked the combination on my locker. "It was more like, well, more like she just asked me but it was weird."

"No, she did it on purpose," said Rachel. "And that's just like her."

"Rachel's probably right," said Emma. "But don't worry about it."

"Yeah, I don't shave my legs yet," said Claire.

"And neither do I," said Yumi.

"I just started last summer," said Emma. "But it's not a big deal."

I was glad to have everyone on my side—but I still felt self-conscious. I wore jeans to school, and socks with my tennis shoes, even though it was pretty hot out. I told myself I wasn't hiding my legs. But deep down, I knew the truth. Hopefully my friends wouldn't make the connection, though. Of course, it would be even worse if Taylor realized it. But what other choice did I have?

"Does her underwear really stick out of her gym shorts every day?" asked Yumi.

"Not every day." I glanced at Rachel, who looked away. "I never said every day."

"Still, it's pretty gross," said Emma.

"*She's* gross, so it's fitting," Rachel said with a huff. "Sure she thinks she's all that, but she's really just a giant muffin top wrapped in designer clothes."

"Oh, so fierce!" said Claire. Claire had been calling lots of things fierce, ever since she heard the word on *Project Runway*, her favorite show. As far as I could tell, it could mean awesome, nasty, or way harsh, depending on the context.

Just then I noticed Hannah and Taylor walking toward us. Yumi saw them too, and told us all to shush, which we did.

As soon as they passed us by, Claire whispered, "Fierce!" and the rest of us exploded into laughter. We just couldn't help ourselves.

I guess we were pretty loud because both Hannah and Taylor glanced over their shoulders. Obviously, they knew something was up, but I figured I was safe. No way could Taylor know we were laughing at her.

Still, our eyes met for a brief second and this look of anger flashed over her face. Like somehow she'd figured it out. The thought gave me the chills.

Later on I tried smiling at Taylor in the hallway, like everything was still cool. She just looked away, as if she didn't even know me.

Then when we had to exchange homework in French, Hannah traded papers with Morgan Greely instead of me. I had to switch with Jeremy Lundy, who marked my mistakes with gigantic red x's, leaving my paper a huge mess even though I'd only gotten two answers wrong.

I felt nervous walking into chorus, but I told myself there wasn't any need to. No way could Taylor and Hannah suddenly not like me just because they assumed my friends and I were laughing at them. Okay, true, we were. But they had no way of knowing that. They couldn't have heard our conversation or anything.

Still, as soon as I headed to my seat, Hannah and Taylor looked at each other and laughed. Then when I glanced at them they grinned, but in this evil "we know something you don't know" kind of way.

An ice-cold, icky feeling spread through me.

Obviously Hannah and Taylor had been talking about me. But were they saying something about my legs? Or my friends? Or worse?

Half of me was dying to know.

And the other half was scared to find out.

chapter four
shop till you drop
(out of utter humiliation)

My mom woke me up early on Saturday morning to ask if I was ready to go dress shopping. It sounded like a trick question. I wasn't ready and didn't know if I ever would be. Then again, I wasn't sure I was the only one. The wedding was in five weeks, and last night I overheard Mom and Dweeble arguing about the guest list. On Thursday, they couldn't agree on the invitations, and on Friday, it was the music. They bickered so much these days I kept waiting for them to call the whole thing off. Then I wouldn't even need a dress.

"Just let me sleep for ten more minutes," I said, rolling over.

"Okay." My mom left me alone, but Pepper jumped onto my bed and sniffed my neck, which made it completely impossible for me to go back to sleep.

"Ugh, Pepper. Cut it out."

He barked in my ear. If he wasn't so adorable, I might have been annoyed. Instead, I threw back the covers and got out of bed.

An hour later, we were on our way to the mall.

"So who did you invite to the wedding?" my mom asked.

"What do you mean?"

"You're allowed to invite one friend, remember?"

"Oh right." I yawned, still half asleep. "Um, no one yet, but I'll probably ask Rachel."

My mom nodded. "Is there anywhere you want to go, in particular?" she asked a minute later.

I shrugged and switched stations on the radio, but all I could find were commercials. "It doesn't really matter."

"We'll try the department stores first, then. Do you have a color in mind? I'm thinking something in purple, or maybe blue."

"Okay." I sighed. Normally I don't mind going clothes shopping, but fancy dresses weren't my thing.

Still, once we got to the first store I couldn't help but get excited. There were so many different styles of dresses: long, short, puffy-skirted, and straight. Some were silky smooth and others had beads or lace or both. I picked out a few dresses on my own, but in the end, my mom found the perfect one for me.

It was gorgeous—light blue on top, with a silver skirt. It had a fairy-tale shimmery quality, but not in a little kids' costume kind of way. It was prettier and dressier than anything I'd ever owned.

"What do you think?" I asked, making my way out of the dressing room. The dress felt smooth and silky against my skin. The skirt part ended at my knees, flared at the bottom, and rustled when I walked—in a good way.

Mom only smiled at me.

"It's not too dressy, is it?" I asked, holding the sides and doing a little twirl, just because it was that type of dress—light and floaty.

"Not at all. You're the maid of honor."

"I like it." I turned around to stare at myself in the mirror. The dress looked and felt great for the most part, but the top part wasn't exactly comfortable. It felt tight and looked strange.

My mom must've noticed, too, because she stared at my chest. "What?" I hunched my shoulders forward and crossed my arms.

"No, don't do that," said Mom. "I need to see something."

I dropped my arms to my sides.

Just then a saleslady in a zebra-striped dress came over and asked if we needed any help. She took one look at me and then glanced at my mom. The two of them shared a smile and I'd no idea why.

"What size is that?" asked the saleswoman.

My mom checked the tag. "It's a twelve."

"I'll get the fourteen," she said, walking toward the dresses.

"I've never been a fourteen." I stared at myself in the full-length mirror.

"Well, you're growing up." My mom had the strangest expression on her face.

Before I could ask her why, the saleswoman came back with the bigger size. I tried it on and couldn't see much of a difference, but I felt shy all of a sudden.

"It's a little big in the hips," said my mom, once I walked out of the dressing room.

"But she can't get away with a twelve in the chest anymore," the saleswoman said. "And that's even without a bra."

Whoa. Wait a second. What did she just say?

She didn't.

She couldn't have.

No, that did not just happen.

"I think you're right." My mom nodded.

And my mother actually *agreed* with her?

I couldn't believe this stranger just announced that I needed a bra for everyone in the entire store to hear. Okay, yes, we were the only people in the dressing area, and she didn't exactly scream it, but still. You never know who could be lurking around the corner.

I darted back into the dressing room and changed into my regular clothes. Suddenly, the dress didn't seem so perfect. Suddenly, it seemed like the most hideous dress in the entire store, so I left it in a ball on the floor.

"Where is it?" asked my mom, when I came back outside empty-handed. The salesperson, I was happy to see, had disappeared.

I lifted one shoulder, striking my most convincing, completely casual, and not-at-all mortified pose. "I don't really want it."

"Don't be silly." My mom marched into the dressing room and put the dress back on its hanger. "It's a gorgeous dress, and you look beautiful in it."

I bounced on the balls of my feet, itching to get out of the store. The fluorescent lights seemed too bright, the air too stale. "You're the one who said it was too big in the hips."

"We'll get it taken in. The tailor is already fixing my gown."

"You already picked out a dress?" I asked.

"Of course," my mom said.

"Are you wearing one of those things over your head too?" I asked.

Mom looked at me, puzzled.

"The thing that looks like a mosquito net."

"Oh, a veil." She laughed. "No, I'm not. I'll be right back, okay?"

She took my dress to the cash register but I hung back, barely resisting the urge to hide inside the nearest rack of clothes.

"Where's the dress?" I asked when she returned empty-handed.

"They're holding it for us."

"Great. So can we finally get out of here?"

"Not yet." My mom put her arm around my shoulders and steered me toward the back of the store.

Before I knew it we were smack dab in the center of the bra department. Yikes!

I figured this day would come, eventually. I just didn't think it would happen so soon.

A saleslady approached right away. She was an older woman with red-framed bifocals hanging from her leopard-print blouse. What was it with the salespeople and animal prints? Did my mom drag me to some safari-themed store?

"Let me know if you need anything," the woman announced loudly, like a robot programmed to embarrass eleven-year-old girls. Or maybe that was a part of her job training.

Before I could say, "No thanks," my mom announced that we were in the market for some bras.

"For my daughter," she added, pointing to me.

Thanks, Mom. Thanks a lot! I glanced around the store, fearing I'd see someone I knew, but thankfully, the entire department was empty. We're talking ghost town. Like, I wondered if everyone else knew something we didn't.

The woman had me raise my arms so she could wrap her tape measure around my chest. After she checked the number she asked, "Would you like to try one in pink or white? Or were you thinking beige?"

"Um . . ." I glanced toward my mom, who said I'd try all three.

"I'll be right back," the saleslady said, and made good on that promise—unfortunately—returning with an armload of bras. "These are just for fit and style. Tell me which ones you like and we'll get the right color for you. There's lots to choose from, and if you don't want a solid, they come in prints too."

I took them and bolted, and didn't realize my mom had followed me into the dressing room until I tried to close the door behind me.

"I'll just stay a minute and show you how to put it on," she said.

I looked down at the tangled pile. It did seem somewhat confusing. "Okay." I handed one of them over.

She showed me how to put the bra on backward around my waist, hook one side to the other, turn it around and then pull up the straps.

Which I did—and then turned around to stare at myself in the mirror. It looked weird, like two slightly (and I mean very slightly) puffy triangles on my chest. "Do I really need this?" I asked.

"You really do," said my mom.

I sighed. The white was so bright, it looked like I was wearing funny-shaped bandages. I turned to the side, glancing at myself from a different angle. "Maybe the beige one would be better?"

"You'll need more than one," she said.

"Why? How many times are you going to get married?"

"Oh, honey, you'll be wearing a bra every day now. Not just with the dress."

Aaargh!

In the end, she bought me three bras: one white, one pale pink, and one lilac.

After my mom paid for them, she asked me if I wanted to try on the dress again.

"Not really."

"Let me rephrase that," she said. "I'd like for you to try on the dress again. It should look much better now, but we have to make sure. We're running out of time, you know."

"The wedding is over a month away."

"And it'll be here before you know it."

Double aaargh!

Once we finally got home, I heard voices coming from the kitchen. At first I worried Dweeble was talking to himself. Then I remembered his son, Jason, was arriving today.

Great—mini-Dweeb was here. Just what I needed!

I followed my mom into the kitchen, but stopped short in the doorway—completely stunned. Because the guy standing next to Dweeble? He was anything but dweeby.

chapter five
bra-tastrophe

I guess my mom already knew Jason, because she went right up to him and gave him a hug. She had to stand on her tiptoes to do so, because Jason was tall. Not freakishly tall, like his dad—just regular, perfect-height sort of tall.

"Welcome home, Jay," she said.

"Thanks, Jeanie, it's great to be here. Love the new place."

Unlike his dad, Jason had all his hair and it was really nice hair too—long and dark and pulled back into a low ponytail. He wore earrings—one thick silver hoop in each ear. Not a lot of guys can get away with wearing two earrings without looking weird, but this one could. And he didn't just look not-weird in them. He actually looked good. Cute, which was crazy, considering that I was describing Dweeble's son.

"And you must be Annabelle."

Before I could answer, Jason walked up to me and gave me a bear hug. "My almost-stepsister," he said as he squeezed.

I didn't know if I was just supposed to stand there or hug him back, so I kind of half-hugged him and patted his back, accidentally dropping my shopping bag in the process. Yeah, that's right—the one full of bras.

When Jason let go, we both looked at the ground—me horrified; him concerned. He bent down to pick it up and I did too and we bumped heads.

"Yee-ouch!" I yelled, clutching my throbbing skull.

"You okay?" asked Jason. His beautiful eyes crinkled in the corners, like he actually felt my pain.

"Yup. I'm fine." I grabbed the bag and backed out of the room.

"Looks like the shopping was a success," said Dweeble. "What did you get?"

"Um . . ." That's all I could say. Um. Which was perfect.

Jason already thought I was a total klutz. Now I was acting like a mute too.

"Oh, we went dress shopping," my mom said, winking at me.

I mouthed a silent thanks, suddenly feeling bad about how I'd acted at the mall.

"That looks like a pretty small bag for a dress," said Dweeble, since the underwear bag was pretty tiny. Small enough to hide behind my back, which I did, even though it was too late.

"The dress is at the tailor's," Mom said. "But we did find some, um, barrettes for Annabelle's hair."

She turned to me and smiled. "Why don't you go upstairs and put them away."

I nodded, so grateful, then bolted to my room.

I put on one bra—the lilac one, which matched my T-shirt—and shoved the rest of them into my underwear drawer. I checked myself out in the mirror above my dresser. You couldn't see the bra through my T-shirt unless I pulled it tight against my chest, and I wasn't about to do that.

In no hurry to get back downstairs, I flopped down on my bed. The clasp felt lumpy against my back. Mom told me that, pretty soon, I'd get so used to wearing a bra, I'd forget it was on. But somehow I doubted that.

The whole contraption felt weird, and I dreaded wearing it to school on Monday. What would happen when I had to change clothes in PE? Only a handful of the sixth graders in my class wore bras, and Taylor was one of them. What if she noticed mine and made a nasty comment about it? Like, what if I'd picked out the wrong kind? Or what if I did the whole thing out of order, and girls who wore bras are supposed to shave their legs *first*?

Of course, there were other things to worry about at the moment. Things that happened to be right downstairs. I could not believe I met my future stepbrother and could only say five dumb words in his presence. Not that *yee-ouch* was a word, even. And for that matter, neither was *um*.

Just then my mom called me for dinner, so I peeled myself off my bed and headed downstairs.

The only empty seat at the table was right across from Jason. I sat down and tried not to stare, which was more challenging than it sounds. I couldn't help but realize that he was a hundred times cuter than the cutest boy at Birchwood Middle School. He and his dad looked nothing alike, and they didn't sound alike, either. Jason had this cool, casual drawl and he said, "man" a lot. As in, "Oh, man, was my flight long." And "Man, the skiing in Lucerne is incredible."

Since Jason is a vegetarian, he and Dweeble had made vegetable stew for dinner. We had something called couscous on the side. The grains were smaller than rice but bigger than sand and tastier than both.

"My friend Claire is a vegetarian," I said.

"Did she stop eating meat because of the animals or for health reasons?" Jason asked.

"Um, I don't know," I said, shrugging, and suddenly feeling dumb. "I think because of the animals, though. I never really asked her."

"I didn't stop eating meat until I was a senior in high school," said Jason. "It's cool that someone your age would make that decision so young."

I shrugged. "Claire is cool. Most of my friends are."

Omigosh! Why did I say something so dumb? Of course I'd think my friends were cool. Otherwise, they wouldn't be my friends.

"So, Jason, you're in town for a while. Do you have any big plans for your vacation?" asked my mom.

"Not really. I'm just here to chill. Catch up with some old friends, that sort of thing. Switzerland is great and all, but it's so quiet. It gets kind of boring after a while. And there's already snow on the ground, so it's nice to be in sunny Cali."

"Cali?" I asked.

"California," he said with a grin as he spooned more couscous onto his plate.

I'd never heard anyone call California Cali and I liked it. A lot. I took more couscous too, and hoped it didn't seem like I was copying him.

"So, Annabelle. What do you think of Birchwood?"

"Um, it's fine." I shrugged. "You know. It's school."

It's school? Way to wow this guy with my stellar conversational skills.

"I went there, but it was ages ago," Jason continued.

"I know. Dwee—, um, Ted, I mean your dad told me."

"I wonder if you have any of my old teachers. Is Ms. Guzman around? Are you taking Spanish or French?"

Before I could answer him a piece of carrot got stuck in my throat and I started coughing. Mom patted my back but it didn't really help.

I reached for my iced tea but knocked over the glass, and it spilled across the table. Mom gave me her water and I gulped it down. Meanwhile, Jason threw his napkin over the spill before it leaked onto the floor.

Once I could finally breathe again, I noticed everyone watching me.

"You okay?" asked Dweeble.

"Fine," I said. "Just fine." Just hugely embarrassed. With a tomato-red face, probably.

What's wrong with me?

I took another sip of water and then felt something weird on my arm. Something that shouldn't have been there. I looked at my shoulder and noticed some random strap sticking out of my sleeve. Huh? I was puzzled at first—then panicked. Extremely panicked. Why? Um, that would be because of my bra strap. Yeah—my bra strap slipped off my shoulder. And it was still slipping—right out of the arm of my T-shirt.

I tugged it back up with my other hand, but it still felt loose, so I raised my shoulder up, hoping that gravity would work in my favor.

Then I felt the other side start to slip. Or maybe it was my imagination. Just in case, I raised my other shoulder.

Now they were both just about an inch from my earlobes.

Hi, Jason, I'm Annabelle Stevens, the mute, klutzy, neckless wonder.

"Something the matter, Annabelle?" asked my mom. Everyone looked my way.

Was she *trying* to humiliate me?

"Nope. Nothing," I said, shooting daggers at her with my eyes. "Everything is fine, but can I please be excused? I have tons of homework."

"They still give homework at Birchwood? Man, that's a shame." Jason leaned back in his chair and winked at me.

When Dweeble winked it was completely dweeby. But when Jason did, he somehow made it look cool, and not like he had something stuck in his eye.

I couldn't help but smile at him. In fact, I almost winked back but stopped myself just in time. That would've been too dorky. I think.

Instead, I put my plate in the sink and got out of there—fast.

chapter six

It took me forever to get dressed on Monday, since I had to try on six different shirts before finding one thick enough to hide my new bra. After carefully adjusting the straps, I wiggled around in front of the mirror for a few minutes, just to be sure that everything stayed where it was supposed to stay. I also wore my bright yellow Converse All Stars with rainbow-striped laces. Sure my feet were a little loud, but I figured that would keep the focus off my chest.

Unfortunately, my plan backfired before I even made it to first period.

As soon as I got to school I saw Taylor sitting on a bench, sandwiched between two Terrors: Nikki and Jesse.

When I tried to walk by, Taylor did an exaggerated double take—like a cartoon character would—and zeroed in on my shoes, asking, "What are those supposed to be?" Then she turned to Nikki and said, "Did someone forget to tell me about circus day?"

The three of them giggled.

"What are you talking about?" I asked.

Taylor flipped her hair over one shoulder and grinned. "I'm just trying to figure out why you're wearing clown shoes," she said.

Nikki laughed so hard she snapped a rubber band on her braces, which made Jesse crack up even more. Taylor just stared at me, like she was actually waiting for an answer.

I stood there for a moment, stunned and frozen, my mind blank and my legs planted firmly on the ground—like they'd grown roots, or something.

If she were a boy making fun of me, I'd use one of Pepper's dog-training lessons, and in fact, one of them came to mind.

Sometimes dogs act out to get attention. Ignore them until they calm down.

Figuring this wasn't the worst strategy, I walked away.

Before I was even out of earshot, Jesse asked, "Oh my gosh, did you see her face?"

Then the three of them went off again, laughing hysterically.

I wondered if Taylor was right, and it really did look like I was wearing clown shoes. I thought about ducking into the locker room to trade my rainbow laces for the plain white ones in my PE shoes, but that seemed too obvious. I didn't want Taylor to think I actually cared about what she thought—although obviously I did, because I stressed about it all morning.

When Claire told me she liked my shoelaces at lunchtime, I cringed and waited for the punch line. It took a few seconds to remember that Claire was a good friend, and would never make fun of me. "Really?" I asked, just to be sure.

"They're absolutely fierce. Primary colors are totally hot this season."

I trusted Claire's opinion completely, since she cared about fashion so much and always wore cute clothes. Today she had on faded jeans with purple and blue flowers embroidered onto the back pockets—ones she'd sewn herself.

"Taylor said it looks like I'm wearing clown shoes."

Rachel was just sitting down and overheard. "No way," she said.

"Way," I replied, gravely.

"Like her shoes are so great," said Yumi as she unpacked her lunch.

"Forget her shoes, what about her jeans?" asked Rachel. "She wore those same ones three times last week."

"So uncreative." Claire munched on a carrot stick and turned toward Taylor's table. "It makes me sad."

"But she could've washed them." I felt it was important to point this out, since I usually wear my favorite jeans twice in one week.

"Hey, how come you always defend her when she's so mean to you?" asked Rachel.

"I don't," I replied quickly.

Claire must have noticed my concern because she explained that it's okay to wear jeans twice in one week, especially if you wear them on a Monday and then again later in the week—like on Thursday or Friday. But wearing the same jeans three times in one week is overkill, especially if on two of those days you pair the jeans with the same exact top. Which is what Taylor did all the time.

Taylor's crowd—I mean Terrible T and the Three Terrors—sits just two tables over from ours and they have to pass us on their way to the trash can.

The next time Taylor walked by our table, Rachel said all sweetly, "I love those jeans."

Taylor seemed wary at first but still mumbled an unenthusiastic thanks, at which point Rachel said, "At least that's what I thought when you wore them all last week."

"Whatever," said Taylor, which everyone knows is the weakest comeback out there.

We were pretty happy, for about five minutes.

Then Nikki walked up to Rachel, handed her a napkin, and said, "You have something on your face."

"What?" asked a confused Rachel.

Nikki squinted at her. "It looks like spaghetti sauce," she said, and then gasped and pretended to be embarrassed. "Oh my gosh. I'm so sorry. That's just your skin!"

Before Rachel could respond, she hurried back to her table, where her crowd sat, laughing at us.

It was way harsh. Unfair too, since Rachel's skin had cleared up this week. I was going to tell her so, but Rachel got all quiet and serious and stared down at her turkey sandwich, like she wanted to be left alone.

Then lunch ended before we even got the chance to retaliate.

At least Taylor didn't bug me during PE. She was too busy painting her nails. Yeah, only Taylor would polish her nails in class. And she didn't even flinch when our teacher, Ms. Chang, took away the bottle.

"No biggie," she'd said with a shrug. "I'm getting sick of that shade, anyway."

If she wasn't so terrible, I might've been impressed.

I wore a sweatshirt to dinner that night, so if my bra strap slipped off my shoulder, no one would see. But I don't think anyone would've noticed, anyway. My mom and Dweeble were too busy arguing about the wedding. Tonight's topic: food.

"Everyone likes passed hors d'oeuvres," said Dweeble.

"But a cheese and cracker table makes much more sense," Mom said.

Jason grinned at me and rolled his eyes.

I smiled back and wondered why my insides felt warm and melty.

"Maybe we should choose the caterer first," said Dweeble. "What about Sammys Second Helpings?"

"The punctuation is all wrong in their sign." My mom crossed her arms and leaned back. "*Sammy's* should have an apostrophe."

"You're going to rule them out because of shoddy grammar?" asked Dweeble. "Can't you stop being an English teacher for five minutes?"

"Oh, I don't know, Dad," said Jason. "I think she has a good point. It's an attention to detail kind of thing."

"Fine, then what about Famous Dave's?" asked Dweeble.

"If he's so famous, how come I've never heard of him?" asked my mom.

"Now you're just being difficult," said Dweeble.

"Why don't you guys just order a bunch of pizzas and call it a day?" asked Jason.

I laughed—right as I was taking a sip of water— and sprayed it all over the table.

Everyone looked at me.

"Sorry," I said, wiping my mouth. "Can I please be excused?" I stood up, cleared my plate, and got out of there as fast as I could—all the time wondering if I could be more of a spaz.

Back in my room, I decided to take another look at Pepper's puppy-training manual. Even though my technique hadn't worked on Terrible T this morning, I figured there might've been something I'd missed.

Plus, it would be cool to find a way to make my mom and Dweeble not fight. I combed through all the pages but sadly couldn't find a thing that might help.

I did find one chapter I hadn't read before.

🐾 ROLL OVER. WHY? BECAUSE I SAID SO. 🐾
Okay, rolling over isn't exactly a necessary or practical skill, like teaching your dog to make outside, sit, or stay. But that doesn't mean it's not worth learning. Just think about the bragging rights. Sure, my dog can roll over. No problem-o. How fabulously impressive will that sound? Very. Alright-y? So here's how you do it.

This trick was much more complicated than the others. No wonder I'd skipped it when I was first training Pepper. There were six whole steps involved.

First, I had to teach Pepper how to lie down. He already knew that, so I figured I was ahead of the game. Next, I had to get him to stay there. Then I had to take a treat and sort of wave it from one side of his neck to the other. In theory, Pepper was supposed to follow the treat with his eyes, move his head, and in the process, roll over so he could better reach it.

I tried this a few times, but it didn't work out so well. As soon as Pepper saw the treat, he sat up and offered his paw. No shocker, since sitting and shaking was something we did all the time.

"No, Pepper," I said, hiding the treat and starting

over from the beginning. Eventually, I got him to lie down, but every time I pulled out the treat, he sat up and offered his paw again. The longer I refused to feed him, the more spastic he became. Pretty soon he wouldn't even sit. Instead, he just jumped up and tried to get at the biscuit, all frantic, as if he hadn't eaten in a week.

When he started barking, I lost patience and just let him eat.

Oh well. Like the book said, rolling over wasn't exactly practical, and I guess Pepper knew enough tricks.

I put the book away and turned to my homework. I had stuff due in all my classes so it took forever. By the time I finished I was exhausted, so I changed into my pajamas and headed for the bathroom.

Tried to, anyway. When I opened up the door, I found myself face-to-face with Jason. An almost-naked Jason.

He was brushing his teeth with a towel wrapped around his waist. Yes, a towel, and only a towel.

Ack! "Oh my gosh, I'm so sorry!" I yelled, covering my eyes and backing out.

"It's fine," he said. At least I think that's what he said. It was hard to tell, since he was talking with the toothbrush in his mouth.

I slammed the door shut and called, "Sorry," again.

He didn't say anything, but I heard him spit, and then turn on the water. I didn't know if I should stand there and wait, or go back to my room.

I also didn't know why I hadn't knocked. It's not like I forgot about Jason. I just sat across from him for an entire meal and he's not exactly a forgettable type of guy.

So what had I been thinking? And how come I was just standing around now?

I turned, about to head for my room, when the door opened. Jason was on his way out—still dressed in only the towel. His hair hung down loose and damp around his shoulders, curling at the ends in the most adorable way.

"Sorry," I tried one more time, feeling silly for lurking in the hall, like a weirdo. "I was just leaving. I mean, I didn't know how long you'd be but I wasn't listening or anything."

I wasn't *listening*? Did I really just say that? I think I did.

Jason held the door open for me. "Bathroom's all yours."

"Sorry," I said, yet again.

"No worries," he replied as he headed down the hall.

Ha! That's easy for him to say.

chapter seven
microorganism; macro-mistake

Guess what?" Yumi asked at lunch the next day.

"Aliens landed in your backyard," Rachel guessed.

"And they gave you the power to fly," Claire said.

"But you used that power to spy on your cute neighbor," said Emma. "So they took it away."

"And then they got so fed up with earthlings, they flew back to Mars," Claire finished. "Which is too bad, because they were going to bring peace on earth."

"You guys, that's not funny!" Yumi stomped her foot and tried to keep from giggling, which proved to be impossible.

"You're the one who told us to guess," Rachel pointed out.

"Okay, fine. Stop guessing. I'll just tell you. I got a cat."

"I'm allergic to cats," said Rachel.

"I thought you were allergic to dogs," said Yumi.

"I'm allergic to both."

"Is it a sphynx?" asked Claire. "Because sphynx cats are hairless, so then you'd be okay."

"Although not totally okay, because then you'd be stuck with a really funny-looking cat," Rachel said.

"That's a common misconception but, actually, most people with cat allergies are allergic to the dander," said Emma. "And there's no such thing as a cat without dander, I don't think."

"My cat has fur," Yumi informed us. "Really cute fur too. She's gray with black stripes and she has the cutest little meow. I can't wait for you guys to meet her—my first real pet! I'm so excited!"

"What about your fish?" asked Emma.

"Those are my mom's, and they're cool to look at, but there's nothing like having a pet you can actually pet. Annabelle, you know what I'm talking about. Right?"

Yumi waved her hand in front of my face. "Earth to Annabelle."

"Huh?" I blinked and looked around. All my friends were staring at me. "What?" I asked.

"You tell us. How come you're acting so spacey?" Rachel asked.

"Spacey?" I stared at her, completely confused.

She smiled. "You're, like, in a daze. You even repeated the word *spacey* in a super-spacey way. So what's up?"

"Oh, I didn't get much sleep last night." As soon as I told her this, I realized I'd had a hard time sleeping for a couple of nights. Ever since Jason came to stay with us, actually. Just knowing he was right down the hall from me made it impossible to relax.

I guess my explanation was good enough, because my friends went right on talking.

"What's her name?" asked Emma.

"Hiroki Kuroda. I named her after the starting pitcher for the Dodgers."

Rachel frowned. "I still think it would've been cooler if aliens landed in your backyard."

"Maybe Hiroki is an alien cat," said Emma.

"Her origins *are* mysterious," said Yumi. "She just showed up at my dad's office park last week and she wouldn't go away. My dad's boss wanted to call animal control, but my dad said no way."

"He rescued her? How sweet," said Claire.

"I dunno. Sounds like the beginning of some scary movie," said Emma. *"Attack of the Killer Kitty."*

We all laughed.

My friends cracked me up. I wished Jason could see me now, here like this, having fun and being goofy in my normal element. He only knew me as the too-quiet, clumsy kid who spit water like a broken fountain and didn't know how to knock.

A little while later I heard someone say, "Hey, Annabelle."

I looked up to find all my friends standing over the table—their stuff packed away and ready to go.

"Didn't you hear the bell?" asked Rachel.

"Bell?"

Everyone looked at one another, not knowing whether to laugh or to be concerned. "Um, lunch is over," Yumi said, finally.

"Right." I stood up fast. "Of course. I knew that. I totally did."

I threw out my stuff and headed to science. On my way in, I had to squeeze past Tobias and Oliver, who were wrestling in the aisle. Oliver accidentally pushed me into a table. It didn't hurt, and he did apologize, but it was annoying just the same.

Funny that Jason was once a Birchwood Boy. Hard to imagine too. I'll bet he was never this immature.

I hoped I'd get used to having him around soon, so I could actually relax and be myself. Maybe we could even hang out. After dinner last night (before the bathroom incident), he and his dad played some one-on-one in our driveway. Dweeble had asked me if I wanted to shoot hoops too, but I'd said no.

I did watch them from my window, though.

Jason had an amazing jump shot, and he could slam-dunk too.

"Ms. Stevens?"

I heard someone call my name and looked around. Tobias sat to my left and Oliver to my right.

Oh yeah. Class had begun and I was supposed to be paying attention.

"Yes?" I asked.

"Did you do last night's homework?" asked Ms. Roberts.

Uh-oh. Homework? Sure. Of course I did, because I always do my homework. It's just, well, it'd probably help if I actually remembered what that homework was and where I'd put it.

I nodded. "Yes, I did."

"Then please answer the question," said Ms. Roberts.

Question? She'd asked me a question?

"Whenever you're ready. I'll wait." Ms. Roberts sat on the edge of her desk and crossed her arms over her chest.

Some of my classmates giggled and for once, I didn't blame them.

I looked around frantically. Yes, we were in science, but that was about all I could remember. My notebook wasn't even open.

Tobias smirked at me, but Oliver was kind enough to tell me what was going on. "She asked you to define *microorganism*," he whispered.

Oh, right. Now I remembered. I'd looked up all ten of the new vocabulary words last night. Right before I'd walked in on Jason. I rifled through my backpack in search of my list and realized I'd left my entire science folder in my locker. Rats! I looked up, panicked.

Oliver slid his notebook over and pointed to the middle of the page, where he'd defined the word.

I had to squint to make out his messy writing but wasn't about to complain. I took a deep breath. "A microorganism is a living organism that can only be seen with a microscope," I read. "Because it's too small to be seen with the naked boy."

Suddenly the entire class burst out in laughter. Except for Ms. Roberts, who stared at me unkindly.

"What?" I asked, looking from Oliver to Tobias. Their faces were red and their eyes squinty. Tobias laughed so hard his whole body shook. At least Oliver had the decency to try and stay calm. Although I did notice tears of laughter forming in the corners of his eyes.

What's going on? I wondered as I looked down at the definition and scanned it again. I didn't know— wait a second. I didn't say. No, I couldn't have. I didn't. But, yes, I did.

"Naked eye. I mean naked eye!" I yelled.

But that just made everyone laugh harder.

"So sorry," I said to Ms. Roberts.

She just shook her head and said, "That's enough. Time to settle down."

"Nice going, Spazzers," said Tobias.

"Oliver's writing is impossible to read," I said.

"Or maybe you've got other things on your mind." Tobias raised his eyebrows.

"Don't be gross," I said.

"You're the one who said 'naked boy,'" Tobias reminded me.

Yeah, like I'd ever forget!

Jason picked me up after school that day, and he showed up in the coolest car I'd ever seen: a blue MINI Cooper with white racing stripes. It was a convertible and the top was down. He looked as cute as ever with hoop earrings, dark sunglasses, and a blue bandana to hold back his hair.

When Jason noticed me, he honked and waved.

"Who's that?" asked Rachel, who happened to be standing next to me.

"Oh, that's Jason," I said. "Dweeble's son."

"*That's* mini-Dweeb?" Rachel propped her sunglasses on top of her head, so she could get a better look. "He's so cute."

"You think?" I asked, even though I knew he was.

"*Way* too cute to call mini-Dweeb."

"Um, I guess so."

I said bye to Rachel and hurried over to the car. "Hey." I slid into the passenger seat and slammed the door behind me, hoping Jason couldn't see me blush.

"Hey, Anna Banana." He'd started calling me that yesterday. My mom used to but I made her stop three years ago because it sounded silly. Babyish, too. Also, I don't like bananas because they're mushy and they smell funny. Still, when Jason called me that, I liked it. "How was school?"

I shrugged. "Okay, I guess." I sat with my backpack on my lap, and crossed one leg over the other. Since it looked a little weird, I uncrossed my legs. Then I crossed them again but at my ankles. My backpack was on my lap and I thought about throwing it in the backseat, but I'd already moved around so much. I didn't want to appear too squirmy.

"I didn't know you had a car," I said, running my hand along the smooth leather interior—then stopping because I didn't want him to see me petting the passenger seat.

"I don't," said Jason. "It's my mom's, but she's letting me use it while I'm in town. She has another car, so she doesn't really need it."

"Oh." I didn't know much about Jason's mom. Just that she and Dweeble got divorced when Jason was ten. Also, she was a real estate broker, and married to some other real estate broker.

Jason turned up the radio, and I was glad we wouldn't have to talk. Even though I desperately wanted to talk to him, I couldn't think of one thing to say. The ride home seemed extra long, but at the same time, way too short.

As soon as we walked into the house Pepper raced over. But instead of jumping on me, he jumped on Jason, who bent down and scratched him behind his ears.

"That's his favorite spot," I said.

"I think that's all dogs' favorite spot," said Jason.

Great. Way to state the obvious.

"Hey, guess what we did today," Jason said.

"Who?"

"Me and Pepper."

He waited for me to guess, but I hate doing that. "Just tell me," I said.

"Oh, I'll do better than that. I'll show you." Jason looked down at the dog and said, "Pepper, sit."

And Pepper sat, obediently, like he always does.

"He already knew how to do that," I said.

"Yo, man, will you chill for half a second? I'm not done yet."

When Jason laughed, his eyes crinkled in the corners. I glanced at Pepper to keep from staring.

Next Jason had Pepper lie down. Then he said, "Roll over!"

"He doesn't know how to—" I stopped mid-sentence, and watched in awe as Pepper rolled over, like he was some kind of show dog.

As soon as he was right side up again, he stared at Jason, looking very pleased with himself.

Jason pulled a biscuit out of his pocket and gave it to him.

"I can't believe you got him to roll over. That's the hardest trick there is."

"I've got a lot of free time on my hands," Jason said, smiling all bashfully. "It's no big deal."

But it was.

"Let's see it again," I said, wondering if maybe Jason had beginner's luck.

This time Jason didn't even have to make him sit first. As soon as he gave the command, Pepper rolled over.

"Good boy," Jason said, and fed him another biscuit. "Want to try?"

He offered me a biscuit.

"Um . . ." I stalled. I wanted to try. I really, really wanted to, but I figured that the more time I spent with Jason, the more likely I was to humiliate myself—again. So I said, "Sorry. Too much homework," and raced upstairs—stumbling on the first step.

"You okay?" asked Jason.

"Fine," I called, scrambling to my room and slamming the door behind me.

I pulled my social studies book out of my backpack and opened it up, but couldn't focus. I had all this nervous pent-up energy and couldn't sit still.

It's because I had the strangest feeling, like I was forgetting something, or something was missing. Soon I realized that *someone* was missing. My dog.

Usually Pepper followed me around the house. He slept at my feet. And whenever I went upstairs to do homework, he hung out in my room, staring out the window or just napping on my bed. But tonight he was nowhere to be seen.

I closed my notebook, tiptoed downstairs, and peeked into the living room. Jason was watching TV on the couch. And Pepper was stretched out right below him, with his head resting on Jason's foot.

This was nuts! Pepper used to love me the best, but now he had a new favorite person. And the craziest thing about it was, I couldn't even blame him.

chapter eight
going nowhere

When I got to our table at lunch the next day, I found everyone huddled around Emma.

"It finally happened," she told us.

"Yes!" Yumi pumped her fist in the air.

Rachel clapped baby claps.

"Shh! Be cool," said Yumi.

"What's going on?" I asked.

Claire leaned close and explained. "Emma is going out with Joe, the Corn Dog Boy." She sounded like a spy revealing top secret information.

The Corn Dog Boys share our table during lunch, not because we choose to sit near them, but just because that's how it worked out. Basically, they're four sixth-grade boys. They usually don't bug us, but sometimes they try and hog the whole table, or throw food at each other, or burp to the tune of "The Star-Spangled Banner," which is way annoying. Oh— and last month they had a corn-dog-eating contest, which is how they got their name. Except I don't think they actually know we call them that.

"Wow!" I said.

"Pretty crazy, huh?" asked Rachel.

"Totally," I said. But to be honest, I wasn't entirely sure what "going out" meant. Like, where were they going? I knew better than to ask, though. Instead I chalked it up to just one more mysterious thing about going to school with boys.

I sat down, pulled out my turkey and Swiss cheese sandwich, and listened carefully. It didn't take long to catch on. "Going out" meant that Emma and Joe were boyfriend and girlfriend.

I could hardly believe that one of my friends actually had a boyfriend. I was impressed because it seemed so grown up and cool. But then I wondered, did this mean everything would change?

So far it was too soon to tell. Everyone just ate lunch, as usual. Emma sat at one end of the table, and Joe sat at the opposite end, and they didn't even look at each other.

The Corn Dog Boys wolfed down their food fast, as usual, and then went off to play Frisbee in the quad before next period.

Once they were gone, everyone huddled around Emma. "So how did it happen?" Claire asked.

"Well," said Emma. "We sit next to each other in math, and my locker is right above his locker, and we always kind of smile at each other, and I've thought he was really cute since day one. He's got the most adorable smile, don't you think?"

Everyone nodded. I did too, even though I wasn't sure I'd ever seen Joe smile. I'd seen him stuff his face with chips on a daily basis, and he was a champion belcher. But smile? I couldn't recall.

Emma paused to eat a pretzel stick and then continued. "Except he had another girlfriend until last week."

"He did?" I asked.

"Sure, he was going out with Jesse," Rachel told me. "You know, one of the Three Terrors."

I nodded, glancing toward Taylor's table and wondering how I missed this. Jesse was the fourth girl in Taylor's crowd. Not Hannah, of course, and not the one with dark curly hair and braces with purple rubber bands. That was Nikki. Jesse had long, straight brown hair with chunky white-blond streaks. Usually she wore her hair in a high ponytail. Even though she was tiny, shorter than me, even, we called her Jesse the Jolly Green Giant, because she wore something green every single day. Seriously—like she was always celebrating St. Patrick's Day. No one knew why, and she wasn't even Irish. The weirdest thing about her, though, was that she always ate green food, too: seaweed salad, lime Jell-O, or long stalks of celery.

Emma went on. "Anyway, I never knew if he liked me, so I finally asked Yumi to ask Phil."

I'd never heard of any boy named Phil. "Is he one of the Corn Dog Boys?" I asked, peeking toward the boy side of our table.

"No, he and Joe are in Spanish with Yumi," Claire said.

"He's got scruffy dark hair and an earring," said Rachel.

"Oh, okay." I nodded, still a bit unsure of who he was, but hoping it wouldn't matter.

Yumi cut in. "So I asked Phil after school. His baseball team practices next to my softball field, so we see each other all the time. Anyway, Phil said he didn't know, but then the next day, I got this note."

Emma dug around in her backpack and pulled out a piece of paper. It was folded into a tiny triangle, like a miniature football. She wiped the tabletop in front of her with her lunch sack, then unfolded and smoothed out the page.

Hey Emma—Wanna go out? Sincerely, Joe.
P.S.: Did you do the math homework? What did you get for number 7?
(Joe, again.)

His handwriting was tiny and boxlike. Even though the entire note was only three lines long, he'd used a whole sheet of paper.

"It's so romantic," Rachel said.

I studied the note carefully, in search of the romantic part. I wasn't positive, but maybe it had something to do with the fact that he used a red pen?

"That's cool," I said.

"My first boyfriend." Emma refolded the note and carefully placed it in a Ziploc baggie. She pressed out all the air, sealed the bag, and then put it inside her French book.

"You're sure that's clean?" asked Yumi.

Emma nodded. "It just held my pretzels and I dumped out all the crumbs."

I had so many questions: Were they going to hang out after school? Or on weekends? Or both? Was she just breaking the news to us today and having lunch with us one more time, before ditching us to have romantic meals with Corn Dog Joe?

Somehow, Corn Dog Joe and *romantic* didn't exactly work together in the same sentence. I wondered if I should start calling him Joe. But that didn't sound right, either.

"You're so lucky you'll have a boyfriend for Valentine's Day," said Claire.

"If they're still together by then," said Yumi. "February is months away."

Emma gasped. "How can you say that? Of course we'll still be together then. I mean I hope we are." She frowned. "I hope I didn't just jinx it."

"Don't worry," said Rachel. "He's into long-term relationships. Didn't he and Jesse go out for a whole month?"

"Three and a half weeks," Emma said. "And then she dumped him for Oliver."

"Oliver Banks, who's in my lab group?" I asked.

Everyone else nodded.

"She likes his accent," Rachel said, rolling her eyes. "That's what I heard, anyway."

Cute and sweet Oliver and snobby Jesse the Jolly Green Giant were going out? How had I missed all this?

I wondered if everyone else was going to get boyfriends now, too. And if so, did that mean I was supposed to find one? How did someone do that, anyway? I was dying to know, but it's not like I could just ask.

Luckily, no one else in our group mentioned having boyfriends, or wanting boyfriends.

Emma didn't stop smiling all through lunch. Her whole face seemed to radiate with joy, like it was her birthday, or she'd won the state Mathlete competition—again. I was happy for her, but still worried that things would change.

Here's the thing, though. Not much did. We still shared a table with the Corn Dog Boys, and we still ignored each other, for the most part. But every day, after they finished eating and got ready to leave, Joe would smile and kind of half wave at Emma on his way to the garbage can. And Emma would kind of half smile and wave back at him.

It was nice—sweet in a warm-and-fuzzy-feeling kind of way. Things were cool, at least until Taylor and her friends found out about the relationship.

"Is it true that your friend Irma is going out with

Joe Johnson?" Taylor asked me in PE, about a week later. If I didn't count that time she made fun of my shoelaces, this was the first time she'd spoken to me since our leg-shaving conversation.

"Um, my friend *Emma* is going out with Joe. I don't know his last name, though."

Taylor rolled her eyes like I was being difficult on purpose. "He's the guy who eats lunch at your table. The one who sits with Tobias and Erik, right?"

I nodded. "Yeah, that's him."

Taylor flipped her hair over one shoulder, huffed—all dramatic—like she was beyond annoyed and then faced forward.

"What?" I asked, although I probably should've known better.

"Nothing."

I figured that would be it, but a few seconds later, she turned around again and said, "Actually, you should tell her to look out, because I don't think he's over Jesse."

"What?" I asked.

"I'm just saying . . . you should warn your friend, Joe never wanted to break up with Jesse. When she dumped him, he practically begged her to change her mind. There were tears in his eyes. I almost felt sorry for the guy, but at the same time, it was kind of pathetic. You know?"

"Um, why are you telling me this?" I asked.

"I just think Irma should be careful."

"Emma."

"Whatever."

Taylor had to know Emma's name. They'd gone to school together since kindergarten, but I decided to leave that one alone. "Be careful of what?" I asked.

"Everyone is saying Joe is just using Emma to get over Jesse, which makes sense, when you think about it. I mean you know what they say about rebound chicks."

I had no idea what they said about rebound chicks, or even what a rebound chick was. Somehow I doubted it had anything to do with basketball. Or baby chickens.

Just then Ms. Chang blew her whistle and yelled for everyone to quiet down.

Taylor faced forward, leaving me to stare at her back. She crossed her legs and hugged her knees. Her final words just hung there, like her shiny, dangly earrings. Or—more accurately—like a threat.

chapter nine
me-ouch!

I took Pepper over to Yumi's on Saturday afternoon. I was excited about meeting her new cat, but more importantly, I was relieved I could get away from Jason for a few hours. It seemed like whenever he was around I said or did something stupid. Or literally choked. I didn't know what my problem was, but until I figured it out, I decided to avoid him as much as possible.

When I got to her house, she was on the front lawn with Hiroki, her scrawny little kitty, who was missing half her tail.

"What happened?" I asked, pointing.

Yumi shrugged. "No one knows. She just showed up that way."

"Poor girl!" I stopped a few feet away and kept Pepper on a short leash. So far, he was too busy sniffing the ground to even notice Hiroki.

"Are you sure this is a good idea, getting Pepper and Hiroki together?" I asked.

"My cousin has a dog and two cats and they all

get along great. She said the trick is to introduce them when they're young and Pepper is still a puppy, right?"

"Yup." I moved closer, and watched Pepper carefully.

I've learned that you can figure out what kind of mood your dog is in by studying his body language. A curled upper lip is like a warning to back off. When dogs hold their tails up, they're feeling happy and confident. Dogs who tuck their tails between their legs are fearful. If a dog's hair is sticking straight up, it means he or she is on high alert. And when a dog bows down and sticks his butt in the air, it's an invitation to play. And that's exactly what Pepper did, as soon as he noticed Hiroki. He also wagged his tail—another good sign.

So I brought him over slowly, keeping a firm grip on his leash. Yumi was right. Pepper didn't attack Hiroki. All he wanted to do was sniff her neck.

Here's the thing, though. Hiroki attacked Pepper. In a flash the cat hissed, leaped out of Yumi's lap, and landed on Pepper's back.

"Oh no!" I yelled.

Pepper let out a whimper and shook her off. Or I should say Pepper tried to shake her off, but Hiroki dug her claws into Pepper and held on tight. Then, once she landed on the ground she hissed and got ready to pounce again. Luckily Yumi grabbed her before she had a chance to.

"Is he okay?" she asked, as she struggled with a squirming Hiroki.

"I guess so." I checked Pepper's fur. He wasn't bleeding or anything and he acted more shaken up than hurt.

Of course, he wasn't the only one. The whole thing made me nervous. Hiroki seemed sweet and innocent . . . but the way she'd snapped and pounced so suddenly? It was crazy. It all happened so fast. And it was so vicious and one-sided. A surprise attack!

"I'm so sorry," said Yumi. "She got nervous, probably. She's still pretty skittish. I'll bring her inside."

Once Hiroki was gone, I ran my hands along Pepper's back. He seemed okay—he just stared at me with his honey-colored eyes, as if to ask, *Why did you bring me here, anyway?*

It broke my heart. "Sorry, big guy."

"Is Pepper hurt?" Yumi asked when she came back outside. "Can we still take him to the park? I need to warm up my arm if I'm even going to have a chance at making starting pitcher next season."

Yumi liked to practice pitching by playing fetch with Pepper. And he liked it too. As soon as he heard the word *park* he wagged his tail.

"Sure, we can go," I said.

"Cool, hold on. I just need to grab a ball." Yumi headed into her garage and came out a minute later. "I'm so sorry about Hiroki. I knew she was a little skittish, but I never thought she'd attack your dog."

"He's okay," I said.

The park was crowded, like it is every weekend. We played fetch with Pepper until the sun set and we had to squint to see the ball.

By the time we got home, Pepper was panting, but this didn't stop him from barreling straight for the living room as soon as I opened the front door. His new favorite person was home—Jason.

"Hey, Anna Banana. Where were you?" He turned off the TV and stretched. There was a hole in one of his tube socks and his big toe stuck out of it. It was more cute than sloppy, though.

"I took Pepper to meet Hiroki, my friend Yumi's cat."

"Cool. You two have fun?"

"We did, but Pepper didn't. Well, not at first, anyway. He got attacked by the cat."

Jason paused mid-stretch. "Pepper got attacked by a cat?"

I nodded.

He laughed and clapped his hands together. "Man, how very catty."

I didn't know what Jason was talking about. Nor did I appreciate that he was laughing about Pepper's attack. Hiroki could've done some serious damage. Her claws were sharp. "It's not funny."

"Sorry. I wasn't laughing about Pepper. It was just my bad pun. And *catty* is one of the most perfect adjectives in the world, don't you think?"

"I don't know."

"Sorry, I guess it's just my bias. I'm not the biggest fan of cats. When I was a kid, one totally clawed me with no warning, just because I was petting her. So they all seem harsh and spiteful. Catty, if you will."

"I like cats, and Hiroki probably just got scared. Who knows what kind of awful life she had before Yumi adopted her? Plus, Pepper is so much bigger than her. He must look like some kind of monster."

Jason bent down to scratch Pepper behind the ears. "Are you a monster? Are you a monster, little guy?"

He talked baby talk to Pepper, who ate it right up, rolling over onto his belly and gazing up at Jason. Clearly, he'd forgotten all about me by now.

But Jason hadn't. "Hey, want to see something cool?" he asked me. "Come on, Pepper. Let's go."

I followed them to the backyard. "You taught him something else?"

Jason grinned and then looked at Pepper. "Stay!" he said. Then he tossed Pepper's red ball in one direction and his nylon bone in the other.

Pepper sat there obediently, gazing up at Jason like he was totally in love with the guy. (And okay, while I couldn't really blame him, it still totally annoyed me.)

"That's cool," I said, since Pepper never showed such self-control with me. Just this afternoon, he got completely spastic when he realized we were heading to the park.

Jason laughed. "Wait, I'm not done yet." He looked

down at Pepper and said, "Get your ball. Come on, man. Go get your ball, Pepper."

Pepper took off toward his ball, which he picked up and brought right to Jason. "Good boy," said Jason, giving him a treat. He told Pepper to stay, again, and then tossed the ball. "Now go get your bone. Go get your bone."

Pepper took off toward his ball until Jason called, "No, Pepper. Your bone. Get your bone."

Suddenly, Pepper stopped, darted left and actually fetched his bone.

Jason turned to me, beaming. "So what do you think?"

I couldn't believe it. Seriously—it made no sense.

"He actually knows the words *ball* and *bone*?" I asked.

Jason nodded. "Took me the whole week to teach him."

"I didn't even know that could be done."

"It's no biggie," said Jason, with a shrug.

"You're . . . amazing." The words came out of my mouth before I could stop myself, before I realized how ridiculous I sounded.

Jason just laughed. "I'm not, really. It's like I said before. I have a lot of free time."

I headed upstairs, completely mortified again. I tried doing my homework, but couldn't focus. In fact, I couldn't even sit still, so I paced back and forth. My heart felt like it was pounding at about a million beats a second, and I had a major case of Jason on the brain. He was all I could think about. Jason training Pepper; Jason watching TV; Jason grilling veggie burgers in the backyard.

I couldn't figure out what was wrong with me.

Not until the next morning, when I woke up in a panic, because the answer hit me, like a lightning bolt to my brain.

The reason I'd been acting all spacey at school?

My excuse for feeling completely flustered at home?

The fact that I'd been thinking about Jason twenty-four/seven?

And the cause behind my fluttery-feeling stomach whenever he was around?

It's because I had a crush on him. Jason. Yes, Jason, my almost stepbrother. Jason, who's twenty years old, as in nine whole years older than me. Jason, with his beautiful wavy dark hair, and big brown eyes, and deep drawly voice.

He's the last guy I'd choose to like, if I could choose that kind of thing.

This was bad. No, this was a disaster.

chapter ten
crushed

It wasn't fair that my first crush was on someone so old. And someone I was practically related to. Someone I'd actually *be* related to in just three short weeks. I wanted to deny my feelings, but I couldn't ignore the signs.

Whenever I saw Jason, my stomach felt queasy, but in a good way. Like I was speeding toward a roller-coaster loop, and I love roller coasters—especially ones that go upside down. Whenever I headed downstairs, I hoped to run into him. I wanted him to ask me how school was, or what kind of music I liked, or how I felt about having chickpeas in our salad that night. (Had anyone else suggested it I'd have said, "Yuck." But since it was Jason I'd said, "Sure, that sounds delicious.")

But wait a second. Maybe that's just what it's like to have a big brother. Maybe I'm supposed to want to see him all the time. How would I know, since I'd never had one before? It didn't have to be a crush, did it? I needed to investigate and knew exactly where to turn.

After avoiding Jason all weekend, I found Emma at her locker first thing on Monday. "How did you know you liked Corn Dog Joe?" I asked.

Emma's eyes sparkled just hearing his name. "Oh, it's complicated," she said. "I guess it was his smile. The first time I saw it, well, my heart went all melty, and I started feeling feverish. I've always thought boys in braces were super-cute. But Joe's braces look cuter than the rest. It's like his are shinier, and they glint more in the sun."

"Huh," I said.

Jason didn't wear braces. His teeth were perfectly straight and he had the sweetest smile.

"And he dresses so well, too. His T-shirts are always pressed and clean, not all wrinkled and stained like a lot of boys' at school. Haven't you noticed how his jeans always have a perfectly straight crease? He always rolls the cuffs just once, and just three quarters of an inch. I think he actually measures. I want to ask, but I don't want to embarrass him or anything. I know most people would find that dorky but I think it's cool. Like, geek-chic, which apparently is making a comeback. That's what Claire says, anyway."

"That's it?" I asked.

She blinked at me and tilted her head. "What do you mean?"

"Well, um, isn't there more to it?"

"Of course," she gushed. "Most of it can't be put into words, though. I think about him all the time, and it's just this feeling that's hard to describe. Oh, and did you know he has a pet rat?"

"Ew!"

"No, it's cool. They're actually very smart animals," she assured me, as she closed her locker. "He's not a sewer rat or anything. His name is Darwin, and he's got this twitchy little pink nose and the tiniest, softest ears. That's what Joe says, anyway. I haven't met Darwin. I have seen lots of pictures, though, and he's the cutest."

I had a hard time conceiving of how a pet rat could be cute, but she seemed so sure. I just nodded. And then the first bell rang and Emma raced to class.

Braced-faced smiles, creased jeans, and non-sewer rats added up to Emma's crush, which all seemed kind of weird. But at the same time, I could relate. After all, I liked the way Jason ate clementines, peeling off the skin in one long, unbroken curl. I didn't even care that he sometimes left those curls on the kitchen counter.

And another thing? Sometimes when Jason wore a bandana to hold back his hair, he looked like a pirate. Not an evil pirate—just a cute, thoughtful one with a heart of gold. And did I mention that he knows how to juggle? Not just tennis balls or apples. He can juggle a spatula, a banana, and a shoe, all at the same time.

But thinking about all of Jason's great qualities wasn't helping my situation. I needed to make myself snap out of this crush thing. So I decided to come up with a list of excuses not to like him. (Besides the obvious, I mean—that we were about to be related to each other.)

Surely he had plenty of negative qualities. I just wasn't thinking hard enough. As soon as I got to English I pulled out my notebook and started a list.

1) Yesterday, Jason left his wet towel on the bathroom floor.
2) His dad is bald, so that means he will be someday too. I think.
3) He's a vegetarian, and bacon cheeseburgers are my favorite food.
4) He lives in Switzerland. That's too far away. After the wedding, I won't see him again for who knows how long?
5) He sleeps too late and watches too much TV. Although maybe that's just because he's on vacation.
6) He's a boy and all boys are dogs. Well, maybe not all boys are dogs. Maybe it's just middle school boys who have canine-like tendencies.
7) And speaking of dogs-mine likes him better, which just isn't fair.

I read over the list. It didn't really convince me, which was unfortunate.

"Annabelle Stevens," Mr. Beller called.

I slammed my notebook closed and looked up. Mr. Beller sighed, like I'd physically pained him.

"Sorry," I said, grinning sheepishly.

"Sorry is not the correct answer. And I'd appreciate it if you'd humor me and at least pretend like you're paying attention."

I folded my hands on my desk and faced forward, determined to concentrate and not think about Jason at all.

Mr. Beller was talking about our next book report, so I took a few notes. But soon I found myself wondering how long he'd been a teacher here, and if Jason had ever been one of his students. If not, did Jason maybe have a class in this very same room? I wondered how old my desk was. Maybe it's the same one that Jason had. Maybe his gum was stuck to the bottom of it . . .

Okay, that's a gross thought. Hopefully they clean the desk bottoms every year. And maybe Jason doesn't even like gum. I'd never seen him chew it. Was that possible? Does anyone not like gum? How weird would that be? Part of me hoped this was the case so I could add it to my list of reasons not to like him. Although maybe that would fall under the category of vegetarianism, as in "food-related reasons" . . . which maybe shouldn't be a reason at all because who cares? Despite what they tell us in health class. You are not what you eat.

Clearly, not thinking about Jason wasn't working out so well. But at least I managed to get through the entire morning without embarrassing myself (again).

By the time I got to science, I had a new plan. I figured I was going about things in the wrong way, just trying to shake my crush. Like Emma said, the feelings were hard to describe. They were just there, and they weren't going away. So maybe what I needed was a replacement crush. Someone to transfer my feelings to. If I could find someone else to like, someone more appropriate, someone in my grade, for instance, then all my problems would be solved.

I stared at Oliver. I'd always thought he was cute, and I had to admit he was nice—for a boy—and the right age. We were in the same lab group and sat next to each other, so it would be easy to pass notes back and forth. But what would I write in a note to Oliver? My mind was blank, which clearly meant I didn't like him. I mean, I *liked* him but I didn't *like* him like him. Plus, he was still going out with Jesse. Things between my crowd and Taylor's were bad enough. I didn't want to give them another reason to hate us.

I looked to my left. Tobias wasn't even a candidate. The guy was too annoying to like, and not cute at all. Still, there were other boys in class. The table behind us was full of them. I turned around to look. Jonathan was cleaning his glasses with the bottom of his T-shirt. He had floppy blond hair and nice brown eyes. Not as deep and soulful as Jason's eyes, but they had potential.

"Um, do you have a staring problem?" he asked me.

Aaargh!

I turned back around without answering him. Middle school boys were so immature! This would never work.

chapter eleven
being green

A whole week went by and I still hadn't found a new boy to like. But unfortunately, it seemed like maybe someone else had. My friends and I were minding our own business at lunch on Wednesday, when Taylor and Jesse, the Jolly Green Giant walked—no, strutted—by.

They kept talking to one another, and didn't even glance our way. Someone who didn't know any better would assume they didn't notice we were there. But they *didn't* look at us in such an obvious way; we knew they saw us and were doing it on purpose.

They stopped at the other end of our table, right behind Corn Dog Joe.

Jesse seemed hesitant, but Taylor sort of shoved her and said, "Give it to him."

So Jesse tapped him on the shoulder and handed him a note.

Joe smiled up at Jesse, like they were friends or something, and then shoved the note into his back pocket without reading it.

Then they headed back to their table. Although this time? When they passed us? Taylor smirked. Like she'd won some game that we didn't know we were playing.

"Um, what was that about?" asked Yumi.

"Yeah, why'd she just give a note to your boyfriend?" asked Claire.

"You don't think she wants to get back together with him, do you?" Emma asked.

"There's no way," said Rachel.

"You know what Taylor said to me in PE last week?" I asked. "That Emma should look out, because Joe isn't over Jesse." I turned to Emma. "She called you a rebound chick."

Emma gasped.

"Wait, when did this happen?" asked Rachel.

"I don't know—maybe a week ago."

"And you're just telling us now?" asked Claire.

"I'm sorry, I didn't really know what—"

"Wait, what did she say, exactly?" asked Emma.

I shrugged. "Something about Joe being heartbroken over Jesse, but I don't think it's true. Joe doesn't seem heartbroken."

We all glanced toward the "boy" end of our table. Joe and the other Corn Dog Boys were making armpit farts.

"He seems okay to me," said Rachel.

"Maybe he's just masking his heartbreak with raunchy behavior," Emma whispered.

"Then that would mean he's been heartbroken for his whole, entire life," said Claire.

Emma bit her bottom lip.

"Don't worry. Taylor doesn't know what she's talking about," said Rachel.

"It's Jesse's fault." Emma huffed. "Jesse and those stupid stalks of celery. I'm surprised her skin doesn't turn green."

We all looked at her, completely confused.

"You know how people who eat too many carrots turn orange?" asked Emma.

"Um, no," said Rachel. "What are you talking about?"

"It's because of the carotene pigment," Emma explained. "When too much of it builds up in your bloodstream, it'll change the color of your skin. The process is called carotenemia."

"And green vegetables do that too?" asked Yumi.

"No, that's just wishful thinking." Emma glanced down at her lunch: tuna sandwich, chips, and apple slices, all in a row. "I don't think it's true, anyway."

"You've gotta wonder what's up with the green thing," said Yumi.

"Maybe she has some rare condition that makes it impossible to digest non-green foods," said Emma.

I shrugged. "Or it could just be some crash diet."

"No," said Claire. "She's always eating green gummy worms. What kind of diet would allow that? I don't know about the food thing, but I have a theory about her clothes. I think she's under the mistaken impression that, fashionwise, green is the new black."

"Could anyone think that?" asked Rachel.

"Well, her unfortunate highlights tell us she's got really bad taste," Claire pointed out.

"You're all wrong," said Rachel. "I think she's a member of some alien race on a secret mission to harvest everything green."

Yumi gasped. "What if she's related to my new cat?"

"She did attack Pepper, out of the blue," I said. "And I could totally see Jesse doing something—"

Rachel grabbed my arm and shushed me, because Jesse was approaching again.

When she passed us this time she gave us a nasty look. Then she whispered something into Joe's ear. Something that made him grin and blush.

"I think I just lost my appetite," said Emma.

"Once more, Terrible T and her Terrors have ruined lunch," Rachel said.

"Forget about lunch," said Emma. "They're ruining my whole life."

We were all totally annoyed, but not just because of how Jesse was flirting shamelessly with Joe. We found lots of other reasons too.

We hated Nikki because she's rich and she lived in a huge mansion in Canyon Ranch and her parents have matching Mercedes convertibles. Yes, her dad owned the town's Mercedes dealership, but that wasn't a good enough excuse.

We hated Jesse because she followed Taylor around and did whatever she said, and she always wore and ate something green. Her blond highlights had dark roots and we were tired of her high pony-tail. She always bopped her head back and forth when she walked to make it swing and Rachel pointed out that this was dumb, and show-offy, and probably bad for her neck, too.

We hated Taylor because she was bossy and braggy and she flirted with too many guys. She gossiped all the time, and her laugh was annoying and kind of fake sounding. She made fun of my cute shoelaces. And fine, maybe Rachel was right all along. Maybe it was obnoxious to brag to the world that you were going to be a huge singing sensation, who'd have sold-out shows on at least three conti-nents, and a mansion in Beverly Hills, and loft apartments in New York, Paris, and Rome.

We couldn't think of a specific reason to hate Han-nah. Rachel said her quietness was the same thing as snobbishness, but I didn't agree. Still, just being friends with Taylor, Jesse, and Nikki was obviously evidence of some serious character flaw.

chapter twelve
turkey-day terror

It was exhausting, hating everyone so much, and I was glad to have a few days off over Thanksgiving break.

Usually, my mom and I go to Seattle to spend the holiday with my uncle, Jake, and his partner, Shane. This year we were sticking around, though not at home. We had to go to Dweeble's friends' house for dinner. Except not Jason. Since he was spending Christmas with us, he was going to his mom's for Thanksgiving. They switched holidays every year. I figured this was a good thing, because the less time I spent around Jason, the less awkward I felt.

It's just too bad I wasn't paying attention when Dweeble told me his friends had a daughter my age. If I'd had a clue about who she was, I would've faked being sick and stayed at home.

Instead, I wound up face-to-face with Taylor Stansfield.

As soon as she opened the front door I took a step back, figuring we'd shown up at the wrong

Thanksgiving—or at least hoping that was the case. But Dweeble acted totally normal, and led my mom inside.

"Hello, Taylor," he said. "Please meet my fiancée, Jeanie. And this is her daughter, Annabelle."

I stayed outside on the front step, hardly believing my rotten luck.

"Oh, I know Annabelle from school," Taylor grumbled.

"What a coincidence." Dweeble beamed down at me, like this was actually a good thing. "You never told me you and Taylor were friends."

Um, friends? Was he kidding? What is it about old people who think that any kids who are the same age and happen to go to school together must automatically be friends? Taylor and I lived in two completely different universes.

Taylor grinned her icy, obviously fake grin.

If this is a nightmare, I'd like to wake up now.

Just then some woman—I'm guessing Taylor's mom, since she looked like an older and less evil version of Taylor—came to the door and gave Dweeble a kiss on the cheek. Then she turned to me and said, "You must be Annabelle. Please come in. I'm sorry about my daughter's manners. She didn't mean to keep you out here in the cold."

Um, somehow I had a feeling that that's exactly what Taylor meant to do.

I walked into the house, which was crowded with

mostly grown-ups, and some little kids. Much to my surprise, Nikki was there, too. Great. Now it was two against one. I was outnumbered.

Even worse, compared to everyone else at the party, I looked like a slob. Our Thanksgiving is always casual, so I was wearing jeans and the T-shirt I'd tie-dyed at Claire's a couple of weeks ago. It never occurred to me to get dressed up. Yet Nikki was decked out in a purple miniskirt with navy blue leggings underneath and gold ballet flats. Taylor had on a short silver dress and high black boots. She looked like a dancer in an MTV video. I hated to admit it, but they both looked totally cute.

I didn't know what to say to them, and they didn't know what to say to me. Clearly none of us was prepared to spend an entire evening together.

Luckily Taylor grabbed Nikki's hand and led her upstairs. The two of them whispered the whole way up. I was glad I couldn't hear what they were saying because it was so obvious they were talking about me.

I followed Mom and Dweeble into the living room, hoping to find some other kids my age. Kids I wasn't mortal enemies with. But all I found were a couple of babies, and Nikki's five-year-old twin brothers building a LEGO castle in the corner.

I sat between my mom and Dweeble and tried to stifle my yawns as the grown-ups all around me carried on another boring conversation about—you guessed it—the wedding.

When Taylor's mom came back into the room to replenish the cheese plate, she asked me where Taylor and Nikki had gone.

"I don't know," I said, figuring she'd just let it go.

"What do you mean you don't know?" She looked around the living room, as if they'd materialize out of thin air.

"Um, maybe they went upstairs?" I said, finally.

"And they just left you here?" I could tell she was upset because the space between her eyebrows scrunched.

Uh-oh. I didn't like the direction this was heading in. "I'm pretty happy hanging out down here." I patted the red and yellow plaid pillow next to me and tried to look comfortable.

"Don't be silly," said Mrs. Stansfield. "Come with me."

I looked to my mom, who was no help at all. "Go ahead," she said.

So I had no choice but to peel myself off the couch and follow Mrs. Stansfield.

Climbing upstairs felt like walking the plank on a ship. Like I was just seconds away from plunging into shark-infested waters. Which, come to think of it, would've been preferable.

Mrs. Stansfield knocked on Taylor's door and then walked in before anyone answered. "Hi, girls. I know you didn't leave Annabelle downstairs on purpose. And I know that you're going to include her in your game now."

"It's not a game. We're playing Wii," Taylor said, all snotty. "Nikki brought over *Rock Band II, Special Edition*. You know—the one I've been begging you for, for months."

"Didn't we just get you that last Christmas?"

"No, that was *Guitar Hero*, which is totally out of date."

"Well, you'll have to make do, somehow," said Mrs. Stansfield.

"And you'll have to live with the fact that you're seriously stifling my music career."

Taylor's mom turned around, and finally noticed I hadn't followed her into the room. "Do you want to join them, Annabelle?"

Trick question. If I said no, would I be able to go back downstairs? Or would that just seem like I was dissing Taylor and Nikki?

I hesitated for too long, which seemed to annoy them. Or maybe it was just my presence.

"Come on in," said Taylor's mom, not leaving me with any real choice.

Taylor and Nikki smiled at me—at least until Mrs. Stansfield left. As soon as the door closed, their smiles turned into sneers.

"This wasn't my idea," I reminded them.

"Whatever," said Taylor.

"I didn't even know Ted knew your parents."

"Hey, you live on Clemson Court, right? Across the street from Rachel?" asked Nikki.

I nodded.

"What's your address?" she asked.

"Number eighteen," I said. "How come?"

Nikki grinned. "I used to live in that house when I was little. Before we moved to Canyon Ranch."

"Really?" I asked.

Nikki nodded. "It's such a cute little place."

"Cute" might have been a compliment coming from someone else. But somehow I knew that Nikki meant cute as in small. It was the way she said it, the tone of her voice. Like she thought she was better than me, just because she lived in a bigger house. Which was dumb but also funny, because if she saw the tiny apartment my mom and I used to share, she'd really act snobby.

I know it was a stupid thing to be upset about, but knowing that I lived in Nikki's old house—her *used* house—annoyed me. At the same time, I wished I were there right now.

Maybe I could pretend I had food poisoning. I'd just eaten three cheese cubes. Is it possible to get sick from cheese cubes?

Taylor turned off the TV and said, "Let's do karaoke instead. *Rock Band* is kind of lame."

Nikki flinched, but cued up the karaoke machine without a word.

"You can go first," said Taylor, handing her the mic.

As "So What" by Pink blared from the tiny speakers, Nikki stood up, swayed her hips and held the microphone to her lips. Nikki's voice was okay but not amazing. She did have some good dance moves and she was an excellent high-kicker. Not that I'd say so.

As soon as the song ended, Taylor said, "I'm next." She chose a Jonas Brothers song, and she actually sounded pretty good.

Then the two of them sat down and studied the list of songs in the machine. It was annoying sitting there like I was someone's kid sister foisted upon them, or worse—like their audience.

"Let's do a classic," said Nikki. "Like 'Popular.'"

Taylor cued up the song.

"You mean from *Wicked*?" I blurted out, before I remembered my plan to stay silent. "I love that play. I've seen it three times."

"No way," said Taylor. "Tickets are so expensive, I had to beg my parents to take me once. What are you, rich or something?"

"If she was rich, she wouldn't live in that little house," said Nikki. "Even I only got to see it once."

"I'm not rich," I said. "But my mom is good friends with the director of the play and he got us tickets, and I loved it so much, he let me come back twice more. For my birthday last year I took my two best friends, and we got to go backstage and meet the cast and everything."

Nikki and Taylor glanced at each other. They were impressed, I could tell. And I didn't mean to brag. I was only being honest. But I was glad I told them. I know I shouldn't have cared, but I wanted to be more than the nerdy girl they had to hang out with. The one who didn't shave her legs and wore clown shoes.

"How does your mom know him?" asked Taylor.

"They used to date. Like, ages ago. When my mom was in high school. He was her first boyfriend."

"Omigosh. What if they got married!" said Taylor.

"Your stepdad would be the director of *Wicked*," said Nikki.

"Unless they got married years ago. And then he would be your real dad." Suddenly Taylor's eyes got wide. "He's not your real dad, is he?"

I shook my head. "No. It's always been just me and my mom. Except for now, since she's marrying Ted."

As I said it, I realized things would never be just me and my mom again.

"I love weddings," said Taylor. "What are you wearing?"

"I got this blue dress that has sheer sleeves and a shimmery skirt."

"Sounds fancy," said Nikki.

I nodded. "It is, because I'm the maid of honor, actually."

"That's so cool!" Nikki practically squealed.

I looked at them, trying to figure out if they were being sarcastic or what. It didn't seem that way. It was more like they'd forgotten they were supposed to hate me. "You think?" I asked.

"Um, yeah," said Taylor, like I was crazy for even having to ask. "It's like the biggest honor there is."

"So, can we meet him?" asked Nikki.

"Ted?" I asked. "Sure, he's right downstairs. But I thought you already—"

"She means the director," Taylor said, impatiently.

"Oh, Mark. He's traveling with the show. They're doing *Wicked* all over Europe now."

"When's he coming back?" asked Taylor.

"I don't know. He was only in LA for the play. Normally he lives in New York."

"I'm moving to New York when I turn eighteen," said Taylor. "Even if I don't have a record contract by then, although I probably will."

I couldn't believe I was sitting here having a regular conversation with these girls that my friends and I had been fighting with for weeks. It didn't seem right. Even though it was kind of nice. Or at least less stressful.

"So now you have to sing with us," said Taylor. She turned to Nikki. "Annabelle's got a great voice."

I smiled. I couldn't help it. All this time I figured Taylor had been too wrapped up in herself to notice that I had a good singing voice too. But she did know.

We sang the song "Popular" together, which was kind of ironic. For me, anyway, since I'm not popular. For them it probably felt natural. When it was through, we moved on to some other songs from the *Wicked* soundtrack.

By the time Mrs. Stansfield called us down to dinner, we were actually having fun. Back downstairs, I didn't know where I was supposed to sit, but Taylor grabbed my hand and brought me to the far end of the table so I could eat next to her and Nikki.

"So where's Jason?" asked Taylor.

"You know Jason?" I asked. My voice rose to a high pitch when I said his name and I hoped that didn't give anything away. The last thing I needed was for Taylor to know about my feelings for the guy.

"Duh!" she said. "Ted and my parents have been friends since forever. I've known Jason since he was a geek with glasses and braces, before he turned cute, even."

I noticed Nikki cringe a little at the braces comment, but Taylor didn't seem to.

More importantly, I had a hard time believing Jason was ever a geek. There wasn't a nerdy bone in his body. But thinking about his body made me blush. And wait a second . . . "You think Jason is cute?"

"I don't think he's cute. I know he is," said Taylor. "Is he coming later or something?"

"He's spending Thanksgiving with his mom," I said. "Since we're having Christmas together."

"Oh." Taylor seemed disappointed but recovered quickly. "You're so lucky to have such a hot brother."

"Stepbrother," I said. "And he's not, yet."

We finished our food way before the grown-ups did and Taylor convinced her mom to let us have pumpkin pie, even though everyone else was still eating their dinner.

Afterward, Nikki and Taylor headed back upstairs.

I didn't know if I was supposed to go too, so I stayed where I was. But then Taylor stopped and glanced over her shoulder and called, "Hey, Annabelle. Are you coming, or what?"

And somehow I knew that "or what" wasn't a real option.

chapter thirteen

I figured Taylor and Nikki wouldn't be mean to me after we'd had so much fun hanging out over Thanksgiving, but I still felt nervous when I got to school on Monday morning, mostly because I didn't know what to expect. I hoped their group would finally get along with my group because I was sick of all the fighting.

But maybe nothing would change. Maybe school would continue to be a battleground, while only home territory was neutral. Maybe even that was wishful thinking. Maybe Taylor and Nikki had already forgotten about how much fun we'd had over Thanksgiving. It was four whole days ago.

As I approached my locker I saw Taylor standing nearby. I didn't want to assume she was waiting there for me, but it did seem that way, so I said hello, although kind of quietly, just in case I was wrong.

"Hola, *chica*," Taylor said, flashing me a wide, bright smile, like we were actually friends. "I thought you might want to borrow this." She handed over a CD—the soundtrack to *West Side Story*.

"Don't tell anyone, but I heard the drama club is doing this for the spring musical. How awesome would it be if I got the part of Maria? They've never given the lead to a sixth grader, but there's a first for everything, right? Anyway, I thought you might want to check it out. Maybe you can try out too. For the chorus."

"Um, thanks," I said.

"Sure. The music rocks. You can keep it for as long as you want," said Taylor. "I already downloaded it to my iPod."

"Great," I said.

"And you should rent the DVD sometime too."

"I will."

"Or come over and we can watch it together, and maybe practice. It would be good to have someone to run lines with."

"Um, okay," I said, hardly believing that Taylor Stansfield actually invited me to her house. Sure, I'd already been there once, but that had been an accident.

"Or I can watch it at your place. Maybe Jason would want to see it too." Just then she looked at her watch and said, "I've gotta motor, but I'll see you in chorus, 'kay?"

"'Kay," I said, and then felt silly because it sounded as if I was copying her. Luckily she didn't say anything and just wiggled her fingers at me before turning to go.

As I was putting the CD in my locker, Rachel came up to me. "What's that?" she asked.

"Um, nothing." I smiled nervously. It was too early in the morning to explain that I was now friends—or at least friendly with—Terrible T. And I didn't know how I was going to either, so I changed the subject. "How was your Thanksgiving?" I asked.

Rachel rolled her eyes. "So boring. We had to go all the way to my aunt's house in San Diego and it took forever. But at least Jackson got carsick and threw up on the way home. That was basically the highlight of the entire vacation." The bell rang. "Gotta run. I'll see you at lunch, though."

" 'Kay." I wiggled my fingers just like Taylor had. It must be contagious or something, because I totally didn't mean to do it.

Rachel tilted her head and asked, "What was that?"

"Nothing." I hooked my thumbs into my back-pack straps.

"Okaaay." She gave me a funny look. "I'll see you later."

"Yup. Sure. See ya."

When I got to French, Hannah said hi to me and asked how my Thanksgiving was.

"Good," I said. "I actually went to Taylor's house. Her parents are friends with my mom's fiancé."

She smiled. "I know. Nikki told me."

This seemed to be code for, "Everything is okay

now, and I can be nice to you, again." Like I passed some test I didn't even know I'd signed up for, which was lucky, because I'd never had any problem with Hannah. And now we didn't have to ignore each other anymore.

"I also heard that your mom is getting married and you get to be the maid of honor," she said. "You're so lucky. I got to be a flower girl once, but that was years ago. Being the maid of honor is much cooler. As long as you like your future step-dad, that is."

"Yeah, he's a good guy. A little dorky, maybe, but nice."

"My dad got married last year and I can't stand my stepmom," Hannah said. "She's a total neat freak. Their house has wall-to-wall white carpet, and no one is allowed to wear shoes inside. She and my dad shuffle around the house in matching beige slippers. Plus, she has a teddy bear collection that she keeps in the living room. It's pathetic. Luckily, I don't live with them, though. I only have to go there every other weekend."

When the final bell rang our teacher asked us to hand our homework forward.

After class, Hannah and I walked out together. We passed Jesse in the hallway, sucking on a lime-flavored lollipop and swinging her ponytail. She said hi to Hannah but not to me. I didn't mind, though, because she didn't roll her eyes or give me a dirty look, or anything. In fact, she didn't seem surprised to see me walking with Hannah. It was like word got out that I was cool. Or at least good enough to be civil to.

I was kind of worried about seeing both Taylor and Rachel in PE, but it turns out that Rachel had to skip her last two classes of the day so she could get braces.

Without her around, it meant I could talk to Taylor without having to explain myself. The thing is—I'd decided that Taylor wasn't anyone I wanted to be enemies with. She was cool and funny and she did this great impression of Ms. Chang, hiking her shorts up past her belly button and walking with her toes turned out and even blowing a fake whistle.

She didn't even seem upset when Ms. Chang caught her and made her run four laps around the football field as punishment—an entire mile. "It's no biggie," she'd said. "I need the exercise."

The next morning Taylor hugged me hello, as if we were lifelong BFFs. She also told me that my hair looked cute.

When she passed me in the hall after first period she said she loved my outfit. I must admit, it was a nice change from being asked why I was dressed for the circus. But the real shocker came at lunch, when she waved me over to her table and said, "Hey, you should eat with us today."

"Um, really?" I glanced toward my regular table, where Rachel and Yumi were just sitting down. Three Corn Dog Boys launched paper airplanes at the other end.

Taylor noticed me looking and grinned slyly. "If you're allowed to, I mean."

Nikki and Jesse laughed while Hannah looked away, pretending not to hear.

"I can eat lunch with whoever I want."

Once I said it I had to ask myself, did I even want to eat lunch with the Three Terrors? Who didn't actually seem so terrible anymore. I mean sure we'd all been in this big huge fight, but everyone deserves a second, er, third, chance, right?

Anyway, it was only one lunch.

A single meal.

Forty-three minutes.

I looked at my friends again. None of them noticed me talking to Taylor and for that I was glad. But what was I so worried about? Why was I making such a big deal out of something so small? And who's to say I can't branch out and make new friends?

"Here." Taylor slid over on the bench seat to make room for me.

Now I had no choice. It would be rude not to join them. At least that's what I told myself, shrugging like it was the easiest thing in the world, as I sat down next to her.

"This is Jesse," Taylor said, jutting her chin out to the Jolly Green Giant, who was busy dipping cucumber slices into ranch dressing.

"Hi," I said, as if I'd never seen her before.

"Hey," she replied, pretending also as she swung her ponytail back and forth.

"And I know you know Nikki and Hannah," Taylor went on.

Hannah smiled at me, encouragingly, while Nikki seemed a little wary.

The cafeteria looked different from here. Their table had more shade and they didn't have to share it with anyone. If my friends asked, I'd tell them I was doing research. Maybe I could write an investigative story for the school paper: *Lunching with the Popular Crowd*.

Or maybe I'd figure out why Jesse was so into the color green.

Winter break was still three weeks away, but she was already wearing a T-shirt with a Christmas tree on it. And it's not like Jesse had that perky Christmas-spirit personality.

Taylor must've noticed me staring because all of a sudden she said, "It's okay to ask her."

"What?" I unpacked my lunch, embarrassed to be so obvious.

Jesse kicked Taylor under the table and widened her blue eyes.

"Cut it out," said Taylor. "Just tell her."

"Really?" asked Jesse. "You promise that won't cancel the whole thing."

Taylor shook her head. "Nope, I promise. Annabelle is cool. She has immunity."

"What's going on?" I asked.

"You're positive?" Jesse seemed worried.

Taylor ignored her and turned to me. "You're wondering why she always eats and wears green, right?"

It's like she read my mind. "Um, I guess I noticed it."

"Everyone notices," Taylor said, prodding Jesse with her elbow. "That's the great thing about it!"

"Ow," said Jesse.

Taylor rolled her eyes. "Oh, come on. I know that didn't hurt. So will you tell her?"

"It's because of Taylor," said Jesse. "She said if I wore and ate something green every day at school for three months—and didn't tell anyone except for our friends—she'd take me to Rosarito with her for Spring Break."

I glanced at Taylor, trying to figure out if this was some sort of joke, but she just sat there looking proud and smug.

"I came up with the idea this summer," Taylor explained. "It's because Jesse hates the color so much. I figured, what could be a better challenge?"

This seemed pretty weird. I didn't know what to ask first. "What's wrong with green?" I finally settled on.

"Gross things come in green," said Jesse. "Brussels sprouts, broccoli, frogs, slime, snot . . ."

"And now you," Taylor said, fake-sweetly as she put her arm around Jesse.

"I'm almost done. Only two weeks to go." Jesse giggled nervously and shrugged away from Taylor.

"I don't think I could do that for three months," I said.

"Not even for an awesome vacation?" asked Jesse.

"Have you ever *been* to Rosarito?" asked Nikki.

I shook my head no.

"It's like, the best place ever," said Taylor. "My parents take me there every year for Spring Break and we always rent a condo, right on the beach. And since I'm an only child and would be totally bored with just them, they let me bring a friend. But only one and it's so hard to decide. Hannah and Nikki have already been, but we've been friends forever. Jesse's still kind of new. We only just started letting her hang out with us last year and she still has to prove herself. But, Annabelle, you can't tell anyone, okay? That's part of the fun. No one else at school can know."

"But why?" I didn't mean to be rude. The question just popped into my head and I really wanted to know.

Taylor and her friends all stared at me. They seemed shocked that I'd asked.

"What do you mean, why?" Taylor asked, carefully.

"Um, why would you make her do that? I'm just curious." I shrugged a tiny shrug. "Why not just let her have a turn."

Taylor smiled. "Well, that wouldn't be any fun! Anyway, it's important to be able to laugh at yourself. You know?"

I glanced toward Jesse, who squirmed in her seat. She wasn't anywhere near laughing. In fact, I'd hardly seen her crack a smile since I'd known her. I'd always figured it was just her personality— or lack thereof. But maybe she just felt super-embarrassed, on account of the fact that she was forced to wear clothes she didn't like every single school day.

The whole thing made me feel uneasy, but I tried to push those thoughts out of my mind. It was flattering that Taylor trusted me with the truth, even though that truth was pretty wacky. None of my friends ever would've guessed that this whole green kick of Jesse's was all because of some bribe. Too bad I couldn't tell them.

"Anyway, if word gets out, the deal's off," Taylor said.

"But that's not fair," Jesse argued. "You said she had immunity."

"She does, but no one else does. I mean where's the fun in that?"

Jesse looked worried.

"I won't tell," I said. "I promise."

"You swear?"

"Pinky swear." I held up my finger.

"I remember pinky swears from the third grade," Nikki said, and laughed until Taylor shot her a dirty look.

"Thanks," said Jesse, as she took a bite of seaweed salad.

"That looks nasty," said Taylor.

Jesse scrunched up her nose. "Well, it tastes even worse."

I glanced at my friends on the other side of the cafeteria. Claire was telling some story that involved lots of arm waving and fake choking and everyone giggling.

"Hey, does Jason have a girlfriend?" asked Taylor.

"Jason Weeble? My almost-stepbrother?"

"Duh." Taylor laughed. "What other Jason is there?"

"Aren't there, like, three in our grade?"

"Four, but none of those guys is worth talking about," said Taylor. "So does he?"

"I don't know."

"Annabelle, how can you not know these pertinent details?"

"Um, I guess it never came up? I never see him with any girls, though. Usually he just hangs out at home with my dog, Pepper. But I guess he could have a girlfriend in Switzerland. How come?"

"No reason. Is he picking you up from school again?" asked Taylor.

"Again?"

"I saw you in the parking lot that day," Taylor said, and turned to her friends. "Jason has the coolest car."

"It's his mom's actually."

"Well, whatever. If he is, can you give me a ride home?"

"You're supposed to come to my house," said Nikki. "My mom is taking us out for manicures, remember?"

"Duh!" said Taylor. "I didn't forget. It's just, if I have the option of seeing Jason, I can't pass that up."

"Not even for a manicure? She said we could get French ones." Nikki turned to me and said, "French manis cost ten dollars extra."

As if I didn't know.

Okay, I didn't, but so what?

"You wouldn't understand. Jason and I go way back. I've known him since forever." Taylor turned to me. "So what's his deal?"

"His deal?"

Just then the bell rang, which was lucky because I'd no idea what Taylor was talking about. And by the time I saw her next, she must've forgotten.

As soon as I got to PE that afternoon, she came up to me. "Isn't it so annoying, how Ms. Meyers never lets us sing good songs in chorus? I'm worried that it's getting in the way of my singing career."

"Um, what do you want to sing instead?" I asked.

"You know—real music that people actually listen to." Taylor flipped her hair over her shoulder. "Pop and hip-hop. Or at least songs from cool musicals like *Wicked* and *Hairspray* instead of boring old *Phantom of the Opera* and folk songs. I'm thinking of starting a petition. Would you sign it?"

"Um, I guess so."

I'd never thought to complain about what a teacher taught and had to admire Taylor for being so bold.

As soon as we split up into volleyball teams, Rachel asked, "Okay, what's going on?"

I played dumb. "What do you mean?"

"Lunching with the enemy?"

"She's not that bad. We kind of hung out on Thanksgiving."

"No way!" Rachel yelled.

"Shh! I didn't know it was going to happen. We just ended up at her parents' house. Her dad and Dweeble went to college together."

"Unbelievable."

"Or maybe they just work together. I don't really know."

"Not that," said Rachel. "I can't believe you got stuck hanging out with Taylor Stansfield and you didn't even tell me."

Yeah, there was a reason I didn't tell Rachel right away. It's because I knew she'd freak out like this.

I shrugged like it wasn't any big deal. "There's not much to tell. She's not so bad. I mean it was weird at first, especially since Nikki was there too. But in the end it was fun."

"How is that possible?" asked Rachel.

"Once you get to know her, she's not so bad." I glanced across the blacktop to where Taylor was talking to Robbie.

Rachel followed my gaze. "He's probably only hanging out with her because he wants to see her underwear."

"Come on," I said.

Rachel shrugged. "Hey, you're the one who told me they're always showing."

"I didn't say always."

"Are you sure?" asked Rachel. "Because I think you did."

I guess I'd said a lot of mean things. But after Taylor made me feel bad about my hairy legs, it had been fun, putting her down. And okay, there was something exciting about getting caught up in the drama. Obviously Rachel wanted to continue this big huge fight, but I didn't want to hold a grudge forever. Anyway, Taylor was nice now.

Just then Taylor looked up, noticed us watching her, and waved. I waved back.

"What are you doing?" asked Rachel.

"Nothing," I said. "Can we play volleyball now?"

"Sure," said Rachel. "And thanks for asking me how I'm feeling."

"Huh?" I asked.

Rachel parted her lips and pointed to her teeth. Her braces! How could I have forgotten? She'd just gotten them yesterday.

"Omigosh, Rachel. I'm so sorry! I totally spaced."

"So I noticed." Rachel huffed.

"Do they hurt?"

"Yes, they do." She crossed her arms over her chest. "Well, they ache a little."

"They look cute," I said.

"Yeah, right."

"No, seriously. Plenty of kids have braces. It's not that big a deal."

"Not for you. Your teeth are perfectly straight."

"How long will you have them?"

"Too soon to tell, but maybe two years if I'm lucky."

"That's not so bad," I said.

"That's forever." Her shoulders slumped. "Jackson's already come up with a huge list of awful nicknames: Train Tracks, Tinsel Mouth, Metal-Mouth Maguire."

"Maguire?"

"They don't have to make sense. They only have to annoy me," said Rachel. "Which they totally do. And as if that weren't bad enough, now you're ditching me for the Terrible T."

"I'm not ditching you and she's not terrible."

"That's what you think," said Rachel. "But just wait."

chapter fourteen
sticky questions

Mom and Dweeble had all their wedding invitations spread out on the dining room table that night after dinner. I picked one up. The paper was thick and cream colored and the edges were soft and frayed—like they'd been torn by someone wearing white gloves and a ball gown.

Seeing the details written out in fancy handwriting made the wedding seem so real, at least until my mom and Dweeble started in, again.

"Do we really have to invite all of the partners at your firm?" my mom asked. "I've never even heard of Davis Patterson."

"Honey, there are only four of us and I can't invite Larry and Brenda without Davis. Anyway, there are plenty of people on your list that I don't know."

The phone rang before they could argue any further, and my mom got up and answered. "It's for you, Annabelle."

"I'll take it upstairs," I said, happy to flee the scene.

"Hello?" I asked, a minute later, sitting cross-legged on my bed.

"Hey, it's Taylor."

"Really?"

"Um, yeah." Taylor laughed. "I forgot my assignment book and I'm wondering if we had any homework in English."

"But we're not in the same class," I blurted out, without thinking.

"I know, but you have Mr. Beller too, remember?"

"How could I forget?"

"You're so funny, Annabelle. You know he gives all his sixth-grade classes the same homework, right?"

I didn't know that, but it made sense. "Hold on. Let me find my assignment book."

When I got back on the phone, Taylor asked, "Hey, I need to ask you something. Do you know if Joe and Emma are serious?"

"Huh?" I asked.

"Well, they've been going out for over three weeks, so I was just wondering . . . Are they serious? Because I know someone else who's really into Joe. I can't tell you who, but she asked me to find out."

I didn't know what to say, so I kept quiet.

"Well?" Taylor pressed.

"I really don't know." This seemed like the safest answer.

She sighed, like this wasn't what she wanted to hear. "I just don't get what they have in common. Emma is so studious and Joe's a total goofball."

"He's not a goofball."

"Well, I know he's smart, but he's also cool, you know?" she asked.

"I guess." I didn't like where this was going. She seemed to be saying that Emma wasn't cool, which put me in a weird position. I felt like I should be defending my friend, but it was hard because Taylor hadn't insulted her, exactly.

"I just don't get what the attraction is. For her, I mean. Don't you think she'd be better off with someone more . . . serious?"

"Joe is plenty serious," I said. "Did you know that he cuffs his jeans three quarters of an inch every day. He actually measures."

"What?" From the sharp tone of Taylor's voice, I realized this was the type of thing I should've kept to myself.

"I thought it was weird at first, too, but when you think about it, it's totally sweet."

"You're telling me that she likes him because of how he cuffs his jeans?"

When Taylor said it, it seemed dorky, but that's not how I'd meant it.

"It's not the only reason she likes him," I said. "It's just one thing that she finds cute."

The silence on the other end of the line made me nervous.

"Look, forget about what I said about his jeans, okay? I probably didn't hear her right."

"Whatever. It's just this other girl I know, she and Joe would be perfect together."

It sounded like Taylor was telling me that Jesse still liked Joe. I thought about the note that Jesse handed him at lunch that day. And how I'd seen them talking in the hallway after math this afternoon. Was something going on between them?

Suddenly I wasn't so excited about this phone call.

"So who do you think is prettier, Emma or Jesse?" Taylor asked.

I didn't want to talk about Emma behind her back, but I had to answer. "I can't really say. They're so different looking." This was true, and better yet— safe. Jesse had dark hair with chunky blond streaks, and blue eyes, and she was short, like me. Emma had naturally dark hair and big brown eyes and she wasn't really tall or short—just average. They're both pretty quiet. But Jesse is quiet and sullen while Emma is quiet and thoughtful.

"I think that since Joe has dark hair, he'd look cute with a blonde," said Taylor. "Or at least with someone who's a partial blonde."

Okay now there was no denying what Taylor was talking about. "But it's not just about looks," I said. "Emma and Joe have a lot in common."

I didn't offer up any more information. Something told me Taylor wouldn't take kindly to the fact that Emma liked the way Joe's braces glinted in the sun. Or that she'd asked Claire to help her design an outfit for Darwin, his pet rat, as a surprise birthday gift. (But whether it was for the rat's birthday or Joe's, I didn't know.)

Luckily Taylor seemed bored with this subject and moved on. "Hey, I almost forgot to tell you. We were talking about you and your friends after school and we all agree that you're the prettiest in the group."

I didn't know *what* to say to that. I was too busy trying to suppress the goofy grin that'd crept onto my lips. Taylor and her friends were the most popular girls in the entire sixth grade. They were the type of girls people noticed. And now they were noticing me. But wait. It didn't seem right, ranking people's looks that way.

"Hello?" asked Taylor.

Woops. I'd been quiet for too long. "Sorry. Um, thanks."

"You're welcome," said Taylor. "Look, that's my other line, so I've gotta motor. But I'll see you tomorrow, 'kay?"

" 'Kay."

It wasn't until I hung up the phone that I noticed my assignment book in my lap. I'd forgotten to give Taylor the English homework. I thought about calling her back, and even reached for the phone, but then I stopped.

Because something told me she never really needed it.

chapter fifteen
mango madness

I had my final dress fitting on Saturday. At least I hoped it was the final one. We'd already been to the tailor twice before, and it wasn't exactly fun or exciting. Besides having to try on my dress and stand there while this lady with big teased-up hair made chalk marks and put pins all over the fabric, I also had to watch her do the same thing to my mom's gown.

There was something good about getting to go, though. My mom and I hardly spent any time alone anymore. And today I needed to talk to her about something important. I waited until we were finished and about to go home, though.

As soon as we put on our seat belts, but before we were moving, I blurted it out. "I think I want to start shaving my legs."

"You think?" My mom glanced at me.

"I mean I definitely do."

"How come?" she asked, as she pulled out of the parking lot and headed toward home.

I slunk down farther into my seat and shrugged.

"Because my legs are hairy," I said. "And because I just want to. It's time."

"Okay," she said, simply. "I'll show you how when we get home."

"It's not like it's a big deal, or anything. Most kids in my grade already shave."

"Most?" asked my mom.

"Well, a lot. More than half, I'm sure. I mean I haven't done a survey, or anything . . ."

My mom smiled, and pulled into the drugstore parking lot.

"I thought we were going home."

"We are. I just need to get you some razors."

Oh right. Wow, this was happening quickly. "You mean I can really do this?" I asked. "Like now?"

She shrugged. "Why not? They're your legs and you're old enough to decide for yourself. And now is as good of a time as any. Ted and Jason are on an all-day hike in Malibu, so we'll have some privacy. We can use my bathroom, since it's got a bigger tub."

"Um, okay." I was glad my mom realized that I couldn't do anything as mortifying as learning how to shave when they were in the house. I'd been contemplating waiting to ask until after Jason went back to Switzerland, but I really wanted to have smooth legs for the wedding, which was only two weeks away.

As much as I wanted to do this, I still felt nervous, knowing it was happening so soon. I half-dreaded having asked in the first place. But at the same time, I was excited too.

Twenty minutes later, I was perched at the edge of my mom's bathtub. I'd changed into my navy blue tank suit because . . . well, just because it made sense at the time. Now I felt silly, but luckily my mom didn't say anything about it.

She sat on the closed toilet seat and tore the wrapping off the razor. It was green with a pink stripe on the handle, and it came with three extra blades. Mom said she'd show me how to change them later.

"The first thing you need to remember is that razor blades are sharp. You always want to shave from your ankle, pulling up. Never move the razor from side to side or you'll cut yourself. And never try to swipe a blade clean with your fingertip. I did that once, when I was your age, and ended up with a sliced thumb. Not fun! Oh, and remember this: the newer the blade, the sharper the edge and you always want a sharp edge."

I shivered, involuntarily. "Um, are you sure? Even for my first time?"

My mom smiled. "I know it's intimidating, thinking about sharp razors, but you're more likely to nick yourself with a dull razor. Okay?"

"If you say so."

"I usually just use soap, but I bought you some shaving cream." She handed me a red can. "Now lather up."

"Which one?" I stared down at my legs, which were sticking out of my suit. They seemed so small and skinny—and not that hairy, even. I sort of felt sorry for them. If you can feel sorry for individual body parts, that is.

"It doesn't matter. We're doing both," Mom said.

She sure was serious about this. I chose my left leg and squirted. The shaving cream came out like funny-smelling whipped cream. I lathered up just past my knee and looked up at her. "How high should I go?"

"That's up to you," she said. "When I was your age, I only shaved to right below my knees, but if you want to go higher, that's okay, too. The knees are a little tricky, though. Since the surface is kind of bumpy, you're probably more likely to nick yourself there."

I decided not to go higher. At least not right away.

Once I finished lathering up, my mom rolled up her pants, held the razor an inch from her leg, and demonstrated what I was supposed to do.

"Just keep your hand steady and try not to move your leg," she said, running the razor from her ankle, all the way up her calf in a straight line. "You only need to apply light pressure."

It didn't seem that hard.

"And don't worry about cutting yourself. If you do, it'll bleed but it probably won't hurt that much."

Of course, now that she mentioned cutting myself, I got super nervous.

"Are you ready?" she asked, holding out the razor.

"Sure." I gulped and grabbed it with a shaking

hand. I put the blade on my ankle. It felt cold but didn't hurt. I took the blade off and checked for blood. It was clean. So far, so good. I took a deep breath and focused on keeping my hand steady. Then I set the blade against my skin, again, and ran the razor lightly up my leg. The blade took all the shaving cream with it, leaving a clean stripe in the center of my leg. A smooth stripe—I couldn't believe how easy and pain-less it was.

"And that's it." My mom turned on the faucet and showed me how to rinse the blade.

Not all of my hair made it down the drain, I noticed. Some of it got stuck to the bottom of the tub.

I made more stripes, shaving until there was no shaving cream left.

Once I finished my left leg, I lathered up my right and managed to shave that one without cut-ting myself, too.

"See, you're a natural," said my mom. "And now you'll have smooth legs for the wedding."

"If there is a wedding," I mumbled.

Mom looked at me strangely. Wait, did I say that out loud?

"Is that some sort of joke, Annabelle?"

"No," I said. "It's just . . . well, you and Ted have been fighting so much . . ."

"What do you mean? We don't fight."

"You do too—about everything: your name, the guest list, the flowers . . ."

"We've never disagreed on the flowers."

"Not yet."

Mom sighed. "Oh, honey, I can't deny that wedding planning is stressful, but these arguments aren't serious. We're not fighting about whether or not we want to be together. I promise. But you can't expect people to get along all the time."

"Well, how about some of the time?"

"We do get along most of the time. You know that." Mom put her arm around me. "Please believe me. Ted and I are very much in love. I wouldn't be going through with this if I wasn't one hundred percent positive that we were ready. Both of us feel this way. You know there are ups and downs in every relationship, right?"

"I guess."

"Is that why you haven't invited Rachel yet? Because you thought we were going to cancel the wedding?"

Actually, I'd completely forgotten to invite Rachel. But I didn't want to make my mom feel bad about that. Clearly this wedding thing was a big deal for her. So I just shrugged.

"Don't worry. We'll get through this ceremony and then things will be back to normal."

I hoped she was right.

Mom left me alone so I could take a shower. I made sure to check the tub for evidence afterward. All those tiny, white-blond hairs were gone, rinsed down the drain, never to be seen again.

After I dried off, she gave me some mango-scented cream for my legs. It left them feeling all soft and silky and smelling like a tropical fruit smoothie.

I took the razors, extra blades, and shaving cream and shoved them in the back of my underwear drawer in my room. Once Jason left, I'd leave them in my bathroom, but until then, well, some things are just too personal.

chapter sixteen
double trouble

I called Rachel later that night and said, "Guess what?"

"Aliens landed in your backyard."

"No, we did that one last time."

"Oh right. Um, let me think for a second. Okay—you traded your family's last cow for three magic beans, and everyone got upset, until you planted them in the backyard and this giant vine grew and then—"

"Close," I said, interrupting. "My mom and Dweeble said I'm allowed to invite one friend to their wedding."

"Oh, cool. Thanks!" said Rachel. Then she paused. "Wait, you were just inviting me, right?"

I smiled. "Of course."

"I've never been to a wedding," she said. "I'll have to check with my mom first, but I'm sure she'll let me go."

Just then I heard someone belch into the phone.

"Cut it out, Jackson," Rachel yelled.

"How'd you know it was me?" He laughed.

"Uh, because no one else in this house is that disgusting?"

"I need to use the phone," he said.

"Well, I'm using it."

"To talk about dumb fairy tales."

"You were eavesdropping!"

"Just hurry up."

"It's okay," I said. "I've gotta go, anyway."

"Okay," said Rachel. "Bye."

I wore jeans again to school on Monday. Not because I was embarrassed about my legs—they were looking nice and smooth. It was more like I didn't want to advertise that I'd started shaving. I didn't want Taylor to think I'd only started because of her comment from a few weeks ago.

It felt weird, putting on shorts at the end of the day for PE. But if Taylor noticed my smooth legs during roll call, she didn't say anything. Our volleyball unit was over, on account of the fact that someone broke into the sports supply room and stole all the nets. So until they got replaced, we'd have to do other stuff. Today we'd warm up with calisthenics and then jog, Ms. Chang announced. We were starting with sit-ups, which meant choosing a partner.

Taylor turned around and asked me to pair up with her.

I wanted to say yes, but then I noticed Rachel staring at me from across the blacktop. She looked kind of worried. "Um, I already promised Rachel. Sorry."

"No biggie." Taylor shrugged.

I got up and walked over to her. Rachel seemed happy enough that I chose her, but it was one of those unspoken things.

"Want to go first?" she asked.

"Sure."

As soon as I got onto my back, Rachel leaned forward and placed her hands on my tennis shoes. "Hey, when did you start shaving?" she asked.

"Just this past weekend. I got fed up with my hairy legs, and with the wedding coming up . . . Well, my dress is short. Not really short. It comes to my knees, but I thought it would be a good idea."

Rachel sort of scoffed. "Um, I hope this doesn't mean you're going to turn into a Taylor clone."

The whistle blew so I started doing sit-ups.

"You shave your legs," I said. "So you can't exactly criticize."

"Well, yeah, but I started because I wanted to. Not because someone told me to."

"No one told me to," I said, but clearly Rachel wasn't convinced.

She glared at Taylor, who'd paired up with Robbie at the other end of the blacktop—out of earshot, I hoped. "I just hate seeing her push people around."

"She's not pushing me around."

"That's what you think," said Rachel. "But you really don't know Taylor."

I sat up, annoyed that Rachel had to make such a big deal out of something so small. Plus, I'd lost track of my sit-up count. "Well, I do kind of know her and she seems nice."

"That's what you think. Taylor is sneaky, and—"

"You make her sound so terrible," I said. "But she's not. And she even wanted to be partners with me, but I told her I wanted to do this with you, instead."

"Oh, and what? I'm supposed to be grateful? Like you sacrificed spending time with the great Taylor Stansfield so you could hang out with me, instead? Thank you so much, Annabelle, but I don't need your pity."

"I didn't mean it like that."

At the sound of the next whistle we switched places and Rachel did her sit-ups in silence.

We didn't speak through the jumping jacks, either.

As we headed to the track to run laps, Taylor ran up to me. "Annabelle!" she cried, grabbing my hand. "I almost forgot to tell you that we got the invitation to your mom's wedding. It's gorgeous. I'm so excited. My mom is taking me dress shopping this weekend. I'm thinking pink. Not bright pink, of course. That would be tacky, especially for a winter wedding. I mean mauve. Although red would be hot. Especially if Jason is going to be there."

I couldn't help but smile. I didn't realize Taylor was invited to the wedding, or that she'd be so excited about it. "That sounds great."

"Can I come over and see your dress?"

"It's still at the dressmaker's," I said.

"Oh. Well then maybe we should get together and figure out how to do our hair," Taylor said.

"Okay, sure."

"Awesome. I'll call you, 'kay?" She waved her wiggly finger wave and took off.

"You invited Taylor to your mom's wedding?" Rachel asked, as we started jogging.

"No, but I guess my mom and Ted did."

"That's so annoying. I can't believe she's going to be there. I wish you'd told me."

"I didn't know, but you'll still come, right?" I asked.

"Well, yeah, I kind of have to. I already told you I would, but it's kind of hypocritical, you know? You hated Taylor as much as we did, and now suddenly she's your best friend?"

I couldn't believe that Rachel was acting like this. "We're not best friends," I said. "And I didn't hate her. I just thought she was snobby, but I didn't know her at all. I'm allowed to change my opinion of someone, aren't I?"

Rachel sighed.

"So, what, you're saying that if I'm friends with Taylor I can't be friends with you too?"

"I never said that."

"But that's how you're acting."

"I'm not acting, at all. I'm just being honest. It's complicated."

"It doesn't have to be. Taylor doesn't care who I'm friends with."

"Then maybe you should just hang out with Taylor," Rachel said.

Suddenly she sped up into a run. I could have caught up to her, if I wanted to. But instead I slowed down.

Obviously Rachel had some big problem with Taylor. But whoever said that the enemy of my friend has to be my enemy, too?

chapter seventeen
roses are red; breakups are blue

Come on," Claire said, grabbing my arm as soon as I got to our lunch table on Friday. "We can't sit here anymore."

I glanced at our deserted side of the table. All the Corn Dog Boys were parked at their end, except for Joe. He was out of sight, and so were Emma, Rachel, and Yumi. I had a bad feeling about this. "What's going on?" I asked, even though I dreaded hearing the answer.

"It's Emma," Claire whispered, waving for me to follow her. "She'll explain."

We hurried to the bathroom, where we found Emma, looking teary-eyed and puffy-faced. A very angry Rachel and Yumi stood on either side of her.

"What happened?" I asked.

Too upset to speak, Emma just blew her nose.

"Joe broke up with her," Yumi explained.

"And he didn't even have the guts to do it in person," said Rachel.

"I found the note in my locker," Emma managed to say between sniffles.

"He broke up with you in a *note*?"

Rachel handed me a wrinkled piece of paper.

The writing was the same, but this time Corn Dog Joe had used blue ink.

*Dear Emma, I've been doing a lot of thinking
and I need to be on my own for a while,
so we have to break up.
From, Joe*

"He signed it 'From' rather than 'Sincerely,'" said Emma—not that she needed to point this out. It was the first thing I'd noticed, after the change of ink color.

"I never realized how much I loved those *'sincerelys'* and now I'll never get to hear one from him again," Emma cried. "Ever!"

Rachel put her arm around Emma. "It totally stinks. I'm so sorry, Emma. He's a jerk. He's worse than a jerk. He's a total butthead."

Emma sniffed. "He *is* a butthead, but I still like him. And now he's back with J-J-J-Jesse." Tears streamed down her face as she blew her nose with a square of toilet paper.

Just then we heard the bathroom door swing open. A girl in red cowboy boots tried to walk in, but Claire hustled her out. "Bathroom is closed. You can't come in."

"But I need to go," she said.

"All the toilets are broken in this one."

Red cowboy boots looked at Emma. "They are not."

"They are. And my friend is just heartbroken over it," Claire said, with a completely straight face.

"Whatever." She rolled her eyes and walked out.

I checked the note, again, completely confused. "How can Corn Dog Joe be going out with Jesse when he said he wanted to be on his own?"

"Exactly. That's the worst part. He wasn't even single for two hours before he asked her out," said Yumi.

"But I thought Jesse was going out with Oliver."

"They broke up after school yesterday. I'm surprised you didn't know about this," said Rachel. "Since Jesse and Taylor have probably been working on this for a while. Probably since Emma and Joe got together."

"Wait. You think they *planned* this?" I asked.

"It's kind of looking that way," said Yumi.

"They never said anything to you?" asked Rachel.

"No!"

"You swear?" she asked.

Claire came to my defense. "Come on, Rach. Of course Annabelle didn't know anything. If she did, she would've told us."

Rachel didn't seem so convinced. She crossed her arms over her chest and glared at me. "So you're saying Taylor never mentioned the fact that Jesse still liked Joe?"

"No," I said, but then I thought back to my phone call with Taylor. She'd never said it outright, but she'd dropped enough hints to make it obvious. Should I have told Emma about that conversation? *Was* this my fault?

Rachel frowned up at the clock. "Emma, you should wash up. It's almost time for next period and you need to let your eyes dry out."

Emma splashed cold water on her face, and dried off with a rough paper towel. "Can you tell I've been crying?" she asked. "I don't want to go to French if everyone is going to know."

Emma's face was flushed and her eyes were glassy. She looked like a wreck, but no one wanted to say so.

"Just tell everyone you have bad allergies," said Rachel.

But that just made her tears start up again.

"Really bad allergies," Yumi tried.

Emma went back to the sink, and turned on the water again, which is why we didn't hear the door opening.

Not until it was too late.

Someone said, "No way! I told her to give it up."

The voice sounded familiar. It was Taylor. Nikki, Hannah, and Jesse were right behind her. A hush fell over the girls' room as we stared each other down.

"Do you mind giving us some privacy?" asked Rachel.

Hannah and Jesse turned to go, but Taylor told

them to hold up. Then she crossed her arms over her chest. "Yes, we do mind. This is a public bathroom."

"There are three more," said Rachel.

Taylor ignored her and looked at Emma, who stood there frozen.

"Have you been crying over Joe?" Taylor's voice was harsher than I'd ever heard it. And she actually laughed. "You're kidding, right?"

"Why shouldn't she be upset?" said Claire. "Jesse totally stole him."

"I didn't steal him," said Jesse, rolling her eyes. "He was perfectly willing to dump you for me."

"But why Joe? You already had a boyfriend," Emma cried.

Jesse shrugged. "And I wanted a different one." She said it so casually, like she was trading baseball cards. "You really need to get over it. It's not like this is a big deal. We were together first and, anyway, Annabelle told us you two weren't serious."

Suddenly all eyes were on me. I felt a sinking feeling in the pit of my stomach.

"I never said that."

"Not to me, but that's what you told Taylor," said Jesse.

"No, it wasn't like that."

Taylor grinned. "Sure, it was. Don't tell me you forgot about our phone conversation. It wasn't that long ago."

Emma stared at me, confused and hurt.

No, this was all wrong. This couldn't be happening. I turned from her to Taylor, frantic. "I said *I didn't know* if they were serious. You know that. Tell them I said that."

Taylor shrugged. "Same difference. If they were serious, you'd know. Believe me. Jesse really appreciates Joe. She's not just some nerd who likes him because of the way he cuffs his jeans."

Emma let out a squeaky, surprised little noise. She sounded like Pepper when my mom accidentally stepped on his tail once. "You told her?"

"No. I mean, not exactly—"

My old friends stared at me, waiting for an answer. But how could I begin to explain?

I couldn't believe Taylor had made me look so evil. That now I was the bad guy. Why did she turn on me?

The first bell rang, but no one moved. It was too silent. I had to make things right.

I looked at Jesse, dressed in black leggings and a Kelly green blouse. How could she have betrayed me when I'd kept her secret? It was so unfair.

Anger flared up from deep within and before I knew it I blurted out, "Hey, know why Jesse wears and eats green all the time?"

"No!" Jesse cried and held up her hands.

I grinned. "It's because Taylor is basically bribing her. She said she'd take Jesse to Rosarito for spring break if she accepted this whole 'Green Challenge' thing, eating and wearing something green every day for three months, straight, without telling anyone. Can you believe it?"

Jesse turned to Taylor. "That doesn't count. I was so close. I only had a few days left. You still have to take me."

Taylor looked from me to Jesse and shrugged. "I don't have to do anything. Rules are rules and you just lost. Guess you can thank Annabelle for that."

Jesse's eyes welled up with tears and she bit her bottom lip. Nikki and Hannah just shook their heads, like they couldn't believe what I'd done. Which was crazy, because they're the ones who'd stolen Emma's boyfriend.

Before I could say another word—not that I had anything to say—they filed out of the bathroom.

Once we were alone, again, I said to Rachel, "That was insane. You were right about Taylor. I never should've trusted—"

"I know I was right about Taylor," Rachel said, and turned an ice-cold gaze on me. "What I didn't realize was that I was so wrong about you!"

"Wait a second." I looked to Emma. "I swear I didn't talk about you like that. Taylor just twisted my words. When I said that thing about Joe, I was defending you."

"But you told her about the jeans," said Emma, in a soft, sad voice that made my heart splinter. "And you said we weren't serious. Why would you say something like that?"

"I didn't mean—"

"Forget it," she said. "I've got to get to class."

"I'm sorry." I turned to Claire. "I don't know how this happened. I just—"

Claire shook her head. "Save it for someone who cares."

I tried reasoning with Yumi. "This was all just a big misunderstanding."

"Really?" she asked. "Well, don't misunderstand this!" She stormed out of the bathroom, and everyone else followed.

I leaned against the wall, stunned and alone. All this time, I'd been stressing over which crowd to hang out with, and now no one liked me.

I'd gone from having eight friends to having zero friends in the span of three minutes.

That's got to be some kind of record.

chapter eighteen
crushed pepper

I hid out in the nurse's office for the entire afternoon. Some might call that wimping out, but I preferred to think of it as surviving.

I figured I'd take Pepper for a walk after school, because he usually cheered me up. But when I got home, I couldn't find my dog anywhere. It's because he was playing fetch with Jason in the backyard.

"Hey," I said.

"Well, if it isn't Anna Banana." Jason looked especially pirate-like in his blue bandana and hoop earrings.

"I was going to take Pepper for a walk."

"Cool, but let me show you his new trick, first."

"You taught him something else?" I asked.

Jason grinned, raised two fingers to his lips and whistled. Pepper bounded over, and sat at his feet, obediently.

"Hey, Pepper," he called. "Let's go for a walk."

Pepper's ears perked up. He looked at Jason and

then darted around the corner, coming back a minute later with his leash in his mouth.

"Amazing," I said. "Pepper, you're a genius!"

Jason laughed.

I bent down and called, "Good boy, Pepper. Come here, genius dog. Let's go for a walk."

Usually just hearing the word *walk* made Pepper go crazy. But today, he acted like he didn't even hear me.

"Come on, Pep. Walk time. I'll take you to the park, if you want."

It's like I wasn't even there. Pepper ignored me completely, because he was too busy gazing up at Jason.

This was too much. I used to be Pepper's favorite person in the house. I'm the one who trained him and I'm the one who took care of him. And now he liked Jason better?

All this time I'd thought Jason was this super-fantastic, amazingly cute guy who made my insides turn to mush. But all that changed in an instant. Now I saw Jason for who he really was: a no-good, sneaky, conniving dog-stealer.

"Want to see him leap through rings?" Jason held up a couple of Hula-Hoops.

"No!" I shouted, and trudged back into the house. Alone!

I tried calling Emma, but her mom said she couldn't come to the phone. When I called Rachel,

Jackson picked up and said she wasn't there. I had this weird feeling he was covering for her, so I waited for a couple of minutes and then walked across the street and knocked on her door.

Jackson answered. "Um, can you say 'stalker'?" he asked.

"Sorry, I thought Rachel might be back by now."

"You just called five minutes ago."

"I know. I just wanted to . . . never mind." I tried peeking into the house, but Jackson blocked my view.

"Do you know when she'll be home?"

"Nope." He slammed the door in my face.

After I crossed the street I looked over my shoulder and caught a glimpse of Rachel peeking out through the living room window.

I tried calling Yumi and then Claire. They either weren't home or—more likely—they were avoiding me as well. Not that I blamed them. Why would they ever forgive me?

I pretended I was sick so I could stay home from school on Friday. My mom was too busy getting ready for the wedding to notice I was faking. And I *did* feel lousy. With no dog and no friends, I was the loneliest loner in town.

There wasn't time to mope around on Saturday. Jason and I had to help out with a bunch of wedding junk—folding programs, moving all the patio furniture aside, and lining up chairs for the ceremony.

Once we were finished, the four of us stood back and surveyed the scene. The place looked amazing, with purple tulips lining the property wall, a dance floor where the patio furniture used to be, and little white lights sparkling in the trees.

"I can't believe that in less than twenty-four hours, you're going to be Ms. Jeanie Stevens," said Dweeble, giving my mom a hug.

She laughed but Jason and I groaned.

"Oh, man, that's a bad joke, even for you," said Jason.

(My mom has always been Ms. Stevens and she wasn't changing her name.)

"Thanks." Dweeble checked his watch. "Almost time for dinner. Who wants to walk Pepper before we go out?"

"I will," both Jason and I said at the same time. "Go ahead," we said next.

He laughed and I started to, but then remembered I was still annoyed that he'd stolen my dog.

"It's cool, Anna Banana. Let me get him for you."

"I'll get him," I grumbled, not wanting him to do me any favors.

But Jason ignored me, raised his fingers to his lips and whistled.

Pepper bounded over.

"Want to make him get his leash?" Jason asked, and then lowered his voice to a whisper. "Just tell him you want to go for a walk."

"It's okay," I said.

"No, you should try it."

I shook my head. "No way. It's not going to work."

"Then tell him to do another trick," said Jason. "Ask him to roll over."

Everyone looked at me, so I had no choice but to try. I sighed and said, "Roll over, Pepper," not expecting anything to happen. But the crazy thing is, Pepper listened to me. It made me happy for half a second but then I caught a glimpse of Jason's smug smile.

"Told you he'd do it," he said.

"Yeah, just because you're here. You don't have to rub it in. Everyone knows my dog likes you better," I said.

Jason blinked in surprise. "He does not."

"Yeah, he does. It's so obvious. You taught him all these cool tricks and he follows you everywhere."

Just then everyone cracked up.

"It's not funny!" I yelled. "How would you guys like getting ditched by your dog!"

"We're not laughing at you," Dweeble said. "It's just, well, there's a reason that Pepper follows Jason everywhere."

"I know—it's because he likes him better."

"No, it's because he keeps dog biscuits in his pockets," my mom said.

"What?" I turned to Jason, who grinned a sheepish

grin. "You mean the only reason my dog has been following you is because you've been feeding him?"

"Of course. You should try it sometime. Works like a charm."

"Actually, you shouldn't," said Dweeble. "Jason, if you keep this up, Pepper could develop a serious weight problem. It's a good thing you're not going to be in town for much longer."

"Um, thanks, Dad."

Dweeble shrugged. "I call 'em like I see 'em."

Meanwhile, I stared at Jason. I can't believe I wasted so many hours worrying about Pepper when, all this time, he'd been swayed by something so small.

I ran to the kitchen and grabbed a dog biscuit, came back and fed half to Pepper. Suddenly he was my best friend again. But what could I expect? He was a dog—a dog with a mind of his own. Yes, it was a fickle mind but he wasn't some object who could be stolen.

It got me thinking about boys.

I mean, it sounds silly and obvious, but it just occurred to me that they had minds of their own too. My friends and I were so mad at Jesse and her crowd for *stealing* Corn Dog Joe, when really, that wasn't possible. It's not like he had no say in the matter.

Too bad I couldn't run this theory by Emma, though. She, like the rest of my former friends, wouldn't return my calls.

But at least I had Pepper.

chapter nineteen

I woke up on the morning of the wedding feeling
pretty jittery. Not about my mom and Dweeble, or
even Jason. I just didn't know how I was going to
face Rachel and Taylor.

What if Rachel tripped me as I made my way
down the aisle? What if Taylor told me my dress
looked dumb—unstylish or babyish? What if the
Rachel-Taylor-Me combination turned out to be completely explosive and ruined the entire day?

Maybe they wouldn't even show up, on account
of the fact that they hated me, and everything. But
that was upsetting, too.

I tried not to think about either of them as I fas-
tened a blue bow to Pepper's collar. He wasn't allowed
outside during the wedding because my mom and
Ted were worried he'd beg for food or dig up the flowers again, but they let me get him spiffed up, anyway.
And that was just one of my jobs.

As the maid of honor I also had to make sure my
mom had everything she needed, which turned out
to be simple. Every time I ask her if she wanted a

glass of water, or a snack, or help with her hair, she said, "All I need is to walk down that aisle and marry Ted Weeble." She sounded so sincere; I wasn't even tempted to roll my eyes. Well, not very tempted.

As I looked at the two of us in the mirror, I couldn't believe this was it. My mom's dress was long and white and flowy. Her hair was swept up in a loose bun, and a few blond curls escaped to frame her face, which glowed. She looked radiant. And to be honest, I wasn't looking so bad myself. My shimmery blue dress fit perfectly. My bra underneath was fully concealed and the straps securely in place. My legs were silky smooth and they smelled like mango. I wore my hair down, with the ends curled up, and I even had on pink lip gloss and sparkly eye shadow.

I was surprised to find that I was excited about the whole wedding and not just that. The marriage would be okay, too. Last night, seeing my mom and Ted curled up on the couch together, making some last-minute changes to their wedding vows I realized something. This whole thing seemed not just good, but right—and not even that big of a deal. Dweeble, I mean Ted, had been in our lives for a long time now. So why not make it more official?

My mom and I grinned at each other. Then she grabbed my hand and gave it a little squeeze. "Okay, I'm ready," she said. "Are you?"

I didn't have to give much thought to my answer. "Yeah, let's do this."

We walked to the back of the house and lined up behind the rest of the wedding party.

Moments later we heard music from the backyard. The string quartet began to play one of those classic wedding songs and I found myself humming along. My insides felt all bubbly, like the champagne all the grown-ups had at dinner last night.

My uncle Jake, who was performing the ceremony, walked down the aisle first. Then Jason, and then Ted, until finally it was my turn. It sounds silly, but they'd had me practice walking so I wouldn't go too fast and for that, I was glad, because as nervous as I felt, at least I had something to focus on: counting steps and breathing.

One, two, breathe.

Three, four, breathe.

Five, six . . . Before I knew it, I was halfway there and looking straight ahead. Wow, it felt weird, being in the spotlight, knowing that all eyes were on me.

When I glanced around, everyone's features blended together. I couldn't make out any single person and I didn't try too hard, either, because all that mattered was right in front of me: my mom, the wedding, and our new family.

Suddenly I found myself standing next to my uncle and across from Ted and Jason. All of them beamed and I did too.

Once I was in place the music changed to something more upbeat and festive. Everyone turned around to watch my mom, who glided down the aisle, like there was no place she'd rather be.

The entire ceremony was short and sweet. One minute, my uncle was welcoming everyone, and the next thing I knew, Mom and Ted exchanged their vows, and kissed, and the entire crowd burst into applause.

After they walked down the aisle, Jason offered me his arm. I placed my hand on his forearm and felt—nothing. No spark or mushiness, anyway— only scratchiness from the wool jacket. And warmth because he was Jason—a nice guy, my stepbrother, who'd maybe teach me how to juggle someday.

"Congratulations," he said, bending down and giving me a hug. "And welcome to the family."

"Same to you." I hugged him back.

"I'm famished. Should we hit the cheese and crackers?" he asked.

"Nah, you go ahead. I'll catch up later."

"Okay. Suit yourself."

Jason headed for the food and I went off in the other direction. Tried to, anyway, but instead I almost ran straight into Taylor.

"Um, hi," I said.

"Great dress," she replied.

"Thanks."

Taylor's dress was pink and strapless and she wore pink eye shadow and pink glossy lipstick to match. "You look nice too. I'm surprised you showed."

"Well, duh. I already bought this dress, and I'm not going to waste it. Plus, we need to talk. Turning on Jesse like you did? Normally, that'd be completely unforgivable, but you actually did me a huge favor, because I didn't want to take her to Rosarito anyway."

"What do you mean?" I asked.

"When I came up with the whole 'Green Challenge' I didn't think she'd actually do it, but she took it so seriously. It was impossible to stop her."

She laughed, nervously, but I couldn't join in.

"So thanks," she went on. "And since Hannah and Nikki have already been, maybe I should take you."

I stared at Taylor, wondering if this was some practical joke. "You want to take me with you on Spring Break?" I asked.

"Maybe," said Taylor. "It's not until April and I'm not going to make the same mistake again. A lot could happen between now and then. But it's a definite possibility. Regardless of that, though, I totally forgive you."

Wait a second. "*You* forgive *me*?" I asked.

"Sure," said Taylor. "But don't ever think about pulling something like that again. Spilling my friend's secret was not cool. But Jesse will forgive you, too, if I tell her to, and anyway, she's too wrapped up in Oliver now to care."

"You mean Joe."

Taylor shook her head. "Um, no. That's old news. Jesse dumped Joe at lunch on Friday."

"But they just got back together."

"Right, but they weren't *together* together. Jesse never really wanted to go out with Joe a second time. I sort of made her, but it's no biggie."

"It's no *biggie*?"

Taylor looked at me like I was the crazy one. "Um, yeah, that's what I said."

"So you're telling me that Emma suffered through all that for nothing?"

"Why do you care? Doesn't she hate you now, anyway?"

I was too stunned to answer, which didn't matter to Taylor because she kept on talking.

"Look, it doesn't matter now, because you can hang out with us. We took a vote after school and it was almost unanimous. So don't worry about Emma or any of those nerds. You don't need them anymore."

My brain was spinning. I didn't know what to object to first. Everything she said was so outrageous, so awful, so *Taylor*. Underneath the shiny hair and beautiful eyes and flawless skin and cute clothes, she was horrible and ugly. I don't know why I didn't see it before but suddenly it all became clear.

Halloween?

That day in PE, when she'd asked me about shaving?

Convincing Jesse to wear and eat green for three months straight, just so she'd take her on vacation?

And a gazillion other examples that had seemed

tiny—not even worth a second thought—until this moment.

Taylor really did think she was better than everyone else. And she actually enjoyed making other people squirm—like everything was some dumb game for her. It was all so cruel. I don't know why it took me so long to figure it out.

"Those aren't nerds. They're my friends."

Taylor laughed. "In what universe are they not nerds?"

"In my universe," I said. "I like them. And they like me. Or at least they did."

"You know, we don't ask just *anyone* to hang out with us."

"Thanks for the offer, Taylor, but I don't want to go to Rosarito with you, or eat lunch with you, or even talk to you, ever. I like my old friends, and if you think they're nerds, well, I guess that means I'm a nerd, too."

I spun around, intent on storming off, but I didn't get very far because Rachel blocked my path.

I wasn't expecting her to show, but there she stood—all dressed up in a lavender dress with blue polka dots and matching ballet flats. Her dark hair hung around her shoulders in tight ringlets. She wore a ton of pink blush. Or maybe she just blushed a ton.

"I can't believe you came," I blurted out.

"Well, honestly, my mom made me, since I'd already RSVP'd."

"Oh." I shouldn't have expected Rachel to forgive me after I'd been such a lousy friend. But I had to try and make her understand. "I'm sorry, Rachel. Everything's so messed up. It was dumb of me to trust Taylor. I should've listened to you from the beginning. I can't believe—"

I was gushing, so it's a good thing she interrupted.

"No, you didn't let me finish. I meant to say—my mom made me come but I'm really glad I'm here, because I heard what you said to Taylor."

"You did?"

She nodded and smoothed out the sash on her dress. "And anyway, it wasn't fair of me to try and boss you around, so I'm sorry too."

My eyes teared up in relief. And I wanted to hug her, but held back because it seemed too soon. "I've missed you."

Rachel grinned. "I've missed you, too. We all have."

"Really? So everyone forgives me?"

"Well, yeah. We talked about it and we decided that you're still kind of new here, so it's not *totally* your fault. And I won't even say 'I told you so,' even though I did warn you."

"I know. I should've listened. She's not Terrible T for nothing."

Rachel smirked and pointed at something going on behind me. "Right, but at least we don't have to worry about her today. Check it out. She's too busy hanging all over your stepbrother."

I spun around and scanned the crowd. It didn't take me long to spot Taylor sitting next to Jason. And not just sitting next to him—she was leaning into him, giggling, tossing her hair over her shoulder, and flirting shamelessly.

Anger flared from deep within me. "I can't believe she's throwing herself at him like that. As if she has a chance. He's twenty years old. In college! It's pathetic. She's such a . . ."

There were lots of things I could've said about Taylor just then. She thinks she's so hot, but she's not, and her friends aren't, either. Her dress is way short and she's wearing too much eye shadow, and with all that pink she looks like a giant frosted cupcake, but the kind that'll make you sick. And aren't cupcakes shaped just like muffins? Which is so perfect. And worse than that, she's the most horrible, phoniest, cattiest person I've ever met.

But that's when this image popped into my brain: Hiroki, Yumi's cat, attacking Pepper out of the blue. She was catty, mean for the sake of being mean. And she wasn't the only one.

Maybe Taylor started this whole feud, but my friends had acted just as badly. So had I.

We'd responded to Taylor's cattiness with more cattiness and everything just grew and festered. Maybe it wasn't any one person's fault. And maybe there was no winning, because honestly? Being mean to Taylor wasn't going to make her less mean and it wasn't going to make me feel any better. Nor was it going to make things right with Rachel and my old friends.

This war between our crowds was no good.

Why should I care if she wants to throw herself at Jason? He's my stepbrother now. This wasn't a competition and I didn't want another reason to fight. I had to be bigger—to not care. Or at least *try* not to.

"She's such a what?" asked Rachel.

I took a deep breath and sighed. "Nothing."

"Nothing?" Rachel looked at me like I was crazy.

"Yes, nothing." I pressed my lips together and blinked, trying to figure out how to explain. "Okay, it's like this. I don't want to be friends with Taylor but I don't want us to be enemies, either. I just want us to be nothing. Can we try nothing?"

Rachel glanced at Taylor and then turned back to me. "But what about Emma?"

"I've been thinking about that. You know how Corn Dog Joe broke up with Emma?"

"The whole school knows that."

"Right, and we blamed Jesse and, by extension, Taylor and her whole crowd. And yes, maybe they had something to do with it. But think about it: *Joe* broke up with Emma, so shouldn't we blame him just a little?"

Rachel grinned with just one side of her mouth, like she wasn't completely convinced. "I was kind of wondering about that, too."

"And if the guy is so wishy-washy, is he even worth getting upset over? Like, maybe we're looking at this all wrong. Maybe Jesse did Emma a favor, because she's probably better off without him. Don't you think?"

"Emma is pretty happy about never having to face his pet rat. Plus, she's sort of into this new guy, Phil."

"Phil?" I asked.

"Yup." When Rachel nodded her curls bounced. "They're both in the physics club. And guess what? He's got a hamster named Einstein."

"Seriously?"

"Yeah, no way could I make that up."

We both smiled.

"Hey, let's go inside and sneak some dessert."

I grabbed Rachel's hand and we weaved through the crowd. When we got to the house I opened up the sliding glass door, not realizing Pepper was on the other side until it was too late.

He pushed past me and barreled out, heading straight for his favorite person.

"Hey, Pepper, come back!" I yelled, but it was too late.

Next thing I knew, I heard Taylor scream. Pepper had pounced on her because she was blocking his path to Jason. And I guess he hit her pretty hard too, because she fell right out of her chair.

I turned to Rachel and cringed. "Yikes!"

Eyes wide, she covered her open mouth with one hand.

We both watched as Taylor stood up and furiously brushed the dirt off her dress.

"Guess you need to step up Pepper's training, huh?" Rachel asked.

"Maybe," I said. "Or maybe he already is trained—really, really well . . ."

"Go, Pepper," she whispered.

I bit my bottom lip, and tried not to smile.

But then Rachel giggled a little. And a little turned into a lot, which was so contagious, we both started laughing like crazy.

And okay, fine. Maybe I should've tried calling Pepper off or gotten Taylor some paper towels or asked her if she was okay. But I didn't. I couldn't because, technically, that would've been something. When I'd just agreed to do nothing. So, really, what could I say?

Nothing.

Except one tiny word that I couldn't resist.

"Meow."

acknowledgments

Special thanks and figurative pats and scratches to:

My family: Judy, Mitchell, Ben, Jen, Dan, Dick, Muggs, Jim, Leo, and Aunt Blanche.

My teen and 'tween consultants: Sydney, Allie, Sophie, Layla, and Julia.

Friends and writers and writer friends: Coe Booth, Sarah Mlynowski, Dan Ehrenhaft, Carolyn Mac-Cullough, Lauren Myracle, Meg Cabot, Ethan Wolff, Jessica Ziegler, and Amanda McCormick.

The fabulous Laura Langlie.

My amazing editor, Michelle Nagler, and the entire Bloomsbury team.

And to everyone who read *Boys Are Dogs* and wanted more from Annabelle.

Don't miss Leslie Margolis's brand-new mystery series!

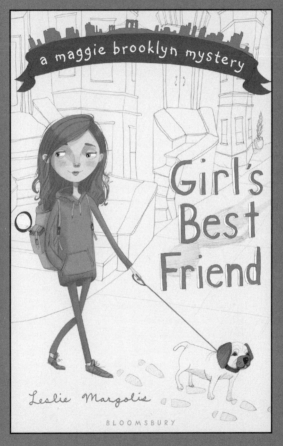

a maggie brooklyn mystery

Girl's Best Friend

Leslie Margolis

BLOOMSBURY

Maggie Brooklyn Sinclair has a twin brother, a secret dog-walking business, and an eye for mystery. Read on for a sneak peek at her first adventure.

Ivy and I used to do everything together: music and ballet when we were little. Fencing and T-ball when we got older. Scrapbook making, modern dance, quilting, origami. . . . All these activities our parents signed us up for. Some fun. Some dumb.

I even helped her pick out Kermit, her first pet—the most adorable black and white Labrador/Dalmatian mutt you've ever seen. We were nine then and Ivy said he could be my dog, too.

We walked him every day after school, taking turns holding his leash.

I helped her give Kermit his first bath—a wet, soapy disaster.

Helped her carry home his first big bag of dog food from Acme Pet Food (before we found out they delivered for free).

He really felt like my dog.

Just like Ivy felt almost like a sister.

Then Eve O'Sullivan's parents had twin boys. They all moved to Brooklyn and everything changed.

At first it was small stuff: Eve and Ivy giggled over stuff that wasn't even funny. They had matching retro rainbow flip-flops and thought it proved they were destined to be friends. More likely, it meant that Urban Outfitters had a sale on flip-flops, but when I pointed this out, they accused me of being jealous.

One day the two of them set up a lemonade stand outside Ivy's building.

I asked if I could help out. They said there wasn't room. And that was the beginning of the end.

The Ivy I knew disappeared—morphed into a different person: a girl who had perfect hair and actually thought that made her better than everyone else.

A girl who wore eye shadow in the sixth grade and real lipstick, not just tinted gloss.

A girl whose socks always matched her shirts, which coordinated with her belts. A girl who made fun of those who didn't get their ears pierced because maybe they were afraid of needles.

A girl who doled out dirty looks the way she used to pass out sticks of gum.

In short, Ivy turned into someone I didn't even know. Someone I no longer even liked. And yet, I still missed her.

But how can you miss someone who doesn't even exist anymore? Two years should have been enough time for me to get over it and move on. And I had, for the most part.

I already knew that Ivy was a lot of things— backstabbing; gossipy; and okay, even pretty mean. But I never knew she was a thief, too.

Yet here she was, taking my stuff.

"Steal from me much?"

Ivy screamed and jumped what seemed like a mile.

"You scared me," she yelled, all accusing—like I was supposed to feel bad.

"Am I supposed to apologize for getting in the way of your robbery?"

"It's not like that," Ivy cried. And that's when I noticed her glassy red eyes. She swiped her shiny tears from her face with the back of her hand.

But were they real? I couldn't tell. There was a time when I'd have given her the benefit of the doubt. Those days were long gone.

"I can explain," she said, staring down at the cash in her hand like she didn't know how it got there.

I walked across the room and grabbed my box out of her hand.

"I can't believe you still have that," said Ivy.

It's not that I'm so sentimental. I swear I didn't keep the cigar box because I was pining over our lost friendship. Rather, the box was one of the coolest gifts anyone had ever given me. It's faded red with a map of the world inside. Musty smelling like it had an exciting history. We used to hide stuff in it when we played Pirates—an elaborate treasure-hunting game we made up. But that was a long time ago.

"It's just a stupid box," I said, opening the lid and checking to see that the keys and all my other dog-walking things were still there.

"I don't need any of that junk," Ivy said. "And I wasn't going to take all of your cash."

"Oh, sorry for the confusion. I should've known you were only going to steal *a little* from me. You know, since it's my birthday and all." I held out my hand and she gave up the stack of bills. I counted it in front of her—figuring it was all there, but knowing it would annoy her.

"I only need some of it and I can explain."

I was so angry I was shaking. "It looks pretty obvious to me, Ivy. First you crash my party and then you try and steal from me? Like it isn't enough to torture me at school every day? You have to come to my house and ruin my weekends, too?"

"I don't torture you," she said. "And the money is for Kermit."

"You're stealing money for your dog?" I asked. "Well, that certainly clears things up. What is it, credit card debt? Poor guy. I didn't realize he was such a big spender."

"Don't be like this, Maggie. I'm serious. Kermit's in trouble."

Ivy pulled a small blue note card from her back pocket and handed it to me. "I wanted to tell you, but I figured this would be easier. And for the record, I was going to pay you back."

I grabbed the note. The printing was so neat it almost looked typed.

> Want to see Kermit again? Bring $100 in an unmarked envelope to the dog beach in Prospect Park tomorrow at noon. Tape it to the nearest park bench and walk away. Make sure you come alone.

"I don't get it," I said.

"Someone stole Kermit and they're holding him for ransom," she said. "And no one else knows—not even Katie or Eve and especially not my parents, so you have to promise me you'll keep quiet."

I glanced at her skeptically. "Is this a joke?"

"No, it's serious." The way her voice broke, the way her whole posture seemed off—anxious, really—made me believe her. "And you can't tell anyone."

"I'm not promising a thing," I said. "But you'd still better explain."

"Fine." Ivy huffed out a small breath in angry defeat. "My parents are in England for two weeks, visiting my grandma because she's sick, and they left me with my other grandma and she was out with her bridge club, so I took Kermit to a stoop sale where I found this very cool top and then I saw a bunch of Diane Von Furstenberg wrap dresses in the window at Beacon's Closet and—" Ivy paused and looked me up and down. "Beacon's Closet is on Fifth Avenue. They sell—"

"I know what Beacon's Closet is."

"Just checking." She held up her hands, all fake innocent.

Ivy's always been way into old clothes and she's got this whole reverse-snobbery attitude about it. She prides herself on finding cool vintage stuff at used-clothing stores and stoop sales and even online. And it is a skill. It's just, I don't know why she thinks this makes her better than other people. Everyone has something they're good at. And for me, it's not fashion. But so what? "I'm not stupid."

"I know. I'm just telling you. It was an emergency. The dress display was adorable, but I had Kermit, so—"

I cut her off. "Did you wash your hands really well after you cleaned up after him?"

"Maggie!"

"I'm just saying. Dogs carry all types of icky diseases." I did my best imitation of her. I couldn't help myself.

"Okay, fine." She rolled her eyes. "I'm sorry, okay? It was just a joke."

"Well, you forgot to make it funny."

"Oh, who cares? No one heard."

"Everyone heard!"

"Everyone?" She raised her eyebrows, all condescending. "I seriously doubt that."

"Everyone in the Pizza Den. Milo, for instance." I didn't want to harp on this, but I couldn't help it. His name just slipped out.

"Well, at least no one good heard."

"What's that supposed to mean?"

"Milo's a dork. He doesn't count."

I started to object but stopped myself. Milo was so much more than a dork, but maybe it was better if Ivy thought of him that way. There'd be less competition. Plus, I didn't want her knowing I liked him.

"Wait a second." Ivy smiled like she could read my mind. "You like him."

"Who?"

"Milo. It's obvious." She clapped and said, "Ha! That's so typical."

"I don't like him," I said, but I couldn't meet her gaze. "And what do you mean by typical?"

"Just that he's totally your type—tall, skinny, floppy-haired. All quiet so you never know what he's thinking. I guess he's not hideous, but he definitely needs a wardrobe update. Have you noticed that sweater he always wears? The one with the big hole?"

"Tell me more about Kermit. What time did you lose him?"

"What?" she asked. "Oh yeah. I tied him up at around three-thirty and he was gone by a quarter to four."

"How did you do it?"

"What do you mean?"

"What kind of knot?"

"I don't know. Square? You know I was always bad at knots in Girl Scouts." Ivy grinned and I had to smile back. We'd both dropped out of Girl Scouts in the third grade—right before we got our rope-tying badges—because Ivy claimed it was a fascist organization. I didn't know what that meant at the time, but it sounded cool, so I kept saying it, too, and eventually our parents got sick of hearing us complain and signed us up for a pottery class instead.

"Anyway, it was only a few minutes," Ivy said.

"Before you said fifteen."

Ivy cringed guiltily. "Okay, I don't know *exactly* how long it was. I guess I sort of lost track."

I shook my head. "I can't believe you left him on the street."

"Do you know how bad I feel? And I already told you it was an emergency . . ."

"A shopping emergency?"

"Yes!" Ivy screamed. "I abandoned my dog so I could shop. I'm a horrible person! I can't even walk by Beacon's Closet without feeling sick."

"Did you see anything suspicious? Or anyone? Do you think someone followed you, maybe? Can you think of anyone who might do this?"

"Like does Kermit have any enemies?" she asked. "He's a dog!"

"I know. I'm just asking. Tell me what happened again. From the beginning this time."

Ivy took a deep breath and huffed. "Fine. So I tied Kermit to a parking meter directly in front of the store, where I'd be able to see him through the window the whole time. Then I went inside and—"

"If you could see him the whole time, then how did he get dognapped?"

Ivy frowned. "I could see him when I was looking at dresses, but the sunglasses display case is in the back."

I groaned.

"It's not my fault," said Ivy. "I made one tiny mistake. In one moment, I had the perfect dress for the fall dance. And in the next, my dog vanished."

"That's horrible," I said. I meant it, too. And in the back of my mind, I also marveled at how she already had an outfit for the dance, which was a whole month away. I had no idea if I was even going. And she'd already figured out what to wear?

I wondered if she had a date. Then I got annoyed with myself for caring.

Meanwhile, Ivy sat cross-legged on my floor, in tears. She seemed so upset I had to believe her.

I handed her a tissue. She blew her nose, loudly, and went on. "I found this cop a block over, and I tried to tell him, but he didn't believe me. I think he thought it was a joke. The way he looked at me—like I was wasting his time. It was awful. And I tried calling the police later on, but they said that dognapping is not a nine-one-one type of emergency and could they please speak to my parents. So I said no and hung up fast. And now Kermit's gone and my parents will be home in ten days and they'll never forgive me."

"You didn't tell your grandma?" I asked.

"No, she's kind of forgetful and she doesn't like dogs. I'm supposed to keep Kermit away from her whenever she's at the house, so I don't even think she's noticed that he's missing."

I hadn't seen Ivy this upset since we got grounded for throwing water balloons out of her window when we were in the third grade. (And to be fair, that had been my idea.)

"But it's not your fault," I said.

"It kind of is. My parents warned me not to tie up Kermit. And they think I buy too many clothes. So this is the ultimate. I didn't know what to do until I remembered what you said about dog walking yesterday. My cousin used to walk dogs when he was in law school and he said it was the best job he ever had. Well paid, too. So I figured you had the cash. I mean, obviously you're not spending money on clothes." She looked me up and down.

"It's amazing how you can ask me for help *and* be insulting at the very same time."

"It's a gift." Ivy shrugged. "But whatever. I'm only stating a fact and you know I'll pay you back. I'm supposed to babysit next Friday and for three Saturday nights in a row. You'll have the money in no time."

Ivy stared at me, desperate. And as much as I wanted to say forget it, I thought of Kermit. One of my favorite dogs in the world, and the one with the saddest puppyhood I'd ever known.

He'd been found in an abandoned building when he was days old. His mom was gone and his whole litter was alone. Two had died by the time the shelter found them. And once we finally convinced Ivy's parents that they must—absolutely had to—adopt one of the puppies, Kermit was the only one left. He had black and white shaggy fur and spots. The skinniest little body you've ever seen—we could see his ribs, even. Huge, fat paws that told us he'd grow up to be enormous. And he did. One time, this kid on the street mistook him for a donkey.

I couldn't believe he was gone.

Despite what Ivy did and despite the girl she'd become, I had to help Kermit. A hundred dollars was a lot of money, but I had it. No way could I refuse.

Still, reading the note gave me the chills. What kind of person would do something like this? No one I wanted to meet.

"I don't think you should go alone," I found myself saying.

Ivy's eyebrows shot up. "But I have to. The note says—"

"I know what the note says, but think about it. It could be dangerous. What if he or she tries to kidnap *you*? Are you sure you can't tell your parents?"

She shook her head. "There's no way."

"Well, what about my parents? They'd help, I bet."

"No, they'll just invoke the parent code and call my parents. You can't say a word." Ivy's cold blue eyes bore into me, letting me know she meant business. She spoke carefully, urgently. "I need to get Kermit back and I need to listen to this person's instructions. So are you going to help me or what?"

I looked down at the note and then back up at Ivy.

I didn't answer right away, but I knew not to argue.

Once Ivy made up her mind there was no going back.

Jimmy Bruch

Leslie Margolis is the author of many books for young readers, including *Boys Are Dogs*, *Girls Acting Catty*, *Everybody Bugs Out*, and *One Tough Chick* in the Annabelle Unleashed series. She is also the author of *Girl's Best Friend* and *Vanishing Acts* in the Maggie Brooklyn Mysteries series. Leslie lives with her family in Los Angeles.

Visit her online at **www.lesliemargolis.com**.